MESMERIZED

Alissa Walser

MESMERIZED

Translated from the German by
Jamie Bulloch

MACLEHOSE PRESS
QUERCUS · LONDON

First published in the German language as *Am Anfang war die Nacht Musik*
by Piper Verlag, Munich, 2010
First published in Great Britain in 2012 by

MacLehose Press
an imprint of Quercus
55 Baker Street
7th Floor, South Block
London W1U 8EW

The translation of this work was supported by a grant from the Goethe-Institut
which is funded by the German Ministry of Foreign Affairs.

ISBN (HB) 978 0 85705 100 4
ISBN (TPB) 978 0 85705 101 1

10 9 8 7 6 5 4 3 2 1

Designed and typeset in Fournier by Libanus Press, Marlborough
Printed and bound in Great Britain by Clays Ltd, St Ives plc

Every sound we make is a bit of autobiography
ANNE CARSON, *Glass, Irony and God*

⊰⊹ CHAPTER ONE ⊹⊱

20 January, 1777

On this winter morning the most famous doctor in the city, his dog in tow, climbs the stairs from the dormitory wing to his treatment rooms. The honey-brown steps can be negotiated with comfortable strides, or it's an easy rhythmical trot for paws. In this house there are no steep and narrow steps. As had been the case in his parents' house. There, he always used to climb down through a gap in the planks to the floor below as if he were on a ladder – apart from when he fell and bruised himself.

He'd rather have stayed in bed, of course. Outside it's pitch black and cold. But he has an important patient to visit, perhaps the most important of his career. He is to examine the blind daughter of the Imperial–Royal court official, Herr Paradis. His wife has requested a house visit. It's because of this step up in his career that he's on his feet so early. And climbing these stairs, which were not designed for the early riser. The extravagant width, the mere hint of a spiral – suggesting a never-ending snail shell – evoke a harmony which can only be appreciated by someone who's enjoyed a good sleep. He has not. It's something of a consolation that Kaline, the housemaid, has already lit the lamps and stoves, but only if she keeps out of sight. If he could just play some music. Since he got married he's been living in this most splendid of houses, with so many rooms that there's even one specifically for his instrument, and yet he cannot play now. A good day always begins with music. Five minutes on his glass armonica is enough. Mozart, Haydn or Gluck, or just running his fingers along the instrument until they find their own melody, and brushing gently over the keyboard like a cat playing in the snow. Then the day will pass in a similarly gentle fashion.

But Anna, his wife, is asleep, the patients are asleep, everyone's asleep, the entire household. Kaline has probably gone back to sleep too. It would be just like her. The moment she sits down – on the kitchen bench beside the range, or on the stool in the washing room – she falls into a deep sleep. Only a couple of days ago he even caught her napping in the drawing room. Reclining on one of the cushions she looked like a tiny animal with closed eyes. Or a slender plant. A flower startled out of its sleep. He would have liked to have gazed longer at her faintly arched eyelids. There's something so innocent, defenceless about closed eyes. But he had to wake her. In a situation like that his wife became loud very quickly, far too loud for an unsuspecting, sleeping girl. He spoke her name, but Kaline did not wake up. He did not want to touch her, so he stood there and started blowing on her face until she opened her eyes. Anna was standing in the doorway, unnoticed, and so it rapidly got loud after all, so loud that sleeping was no longer an option. Her ranting banished all sleep into the furthest corners of the house. Down into the dark vaults of the cellar. And up high, even higher than the servants' bedrooms, up into that minuscule space immediately beneath the roof. A cubby hole that looked as if it had been made from spiders' webs, where the windows were nailed up because of the pigeons. There, sleep was still sleep, this most natural of states for human beings. And the most fitting. After all, human existence begins in sleep. And why did nature conceive human beings if not to sustain her existence? And which state could be more fitting for this than sleep? Mesmer's theory: people wake up to eat and drink so they can go back to sleep without starving. Human beings wake up so they can sleep.

Only he is different. He sleeps to work. He has to be up with the birds, no, well before them. When his day begins no bird is dreaming yet of the sun. And what does sun mean here, what does bird mean? Vienna in January. Neither sun, nor birds. Crows, yes, birds from the raven family. Large blackish-grey Russian crows which in the soupy Viennese fog are hard to distinguish from the grey stone of the houses. And they're forever squabbling over food.

Surprisingly, his wife thinks exactly the same way about sleep as he does. Anna even goes so far as to say that getting up before ten is bad for one's health. And a person in bad health is not to God's liking. And she says this in such a way that not even the empress's personal physician, Störck, would dare meet her gaze. Herr Prof. Dr Anton von Störck. Who is endlessly warning his students about sleep and idleness. And hadn't Mesmer the student found this subject particularly appealing? He, a student and over thirty years old. His doctorate not until he was thirty-three. The eternal student, a type his parents had often ridiculed. And a type they had lumped him in with, too. It wasn't nice. He had, in fact, studied for an eternity. First theology, then mathematics, then law and philosophy, then medicine. The classic combination. Perfect. Nobody could accuse him of laziness. Even though he had always slept well. But Professor Störck does not differentiate between sleeping and lazing around. Just as he does not differentiate between Mesmer's new method and the things dreamed up by occultists, astrologers and charlatans. Störck did accept his doctoral dissertation. Even though he gulped when reading the title. *De planetarum influxu in corpus humanum.* The influence of the planets on the human body. Mesmer explained that it wasn't about horoscopes, but a scientific investigation into the effects the heavenly bodies have on earth. In the end Störck had been reasonably convinced. At least enough to make him put his signature beneath his work. Since then Mesmer had been able to call himself a Doctor of Medicine.

Why was he thinking of Herr von Störck so early in the morning? There could be no more miserable way of starting the day than with the thought of his old professor. A man he once had trusted so much that he'd even made him, on Anna's wishes, a witness at their wedding. Now he'll never be rid of the man. And what's more this thought seldom comes alone. As in real life, unpleasantness breeds with unpleasantness to produce more unpleasantness. Which is particularly unpleasant on the stomach at such an early hour. He thinks of Prof. Ingenhousz from London, the renowned scientist who inoculated against the pox, member of the Royal Academy. He made the following public statement about Mesmer's discovery: *Only the genius of an Englishman would be a capable of making such a discovery, and so there could not be any substance to it.* And now Mr Ingenious is inoculating the Viennese against the pox! Without giving a damn about the consequences. And Dr Barth, the renowned cataract surgeon, and all the rest of them. The entire medical fraternity who refuse to take him, but most of all his new healing method, seriously. Who want to crush him. Thinking about them at this very moment, on this early morning, he thinks, is like poisoning oneself. Thoughts, he thinks, are like medicine. Take the wrong dose and you perish.

He trots through the large treatment room. The dog, delighted by the change in pace, leaps up at him. He fends it off with one hand while the other feels for the key to his laboratory in the pocket of his smoking jacket. And finds a small leather bag – empty. The girl would know where the key is, but where is the girl? If he calls her, he'll wake the entire house. Cursing quietly he makes his way to the back corridor. The laboratory door – it's wide open!

The key to the most secret, most important room in the house is in the lock! On the inside. God only knows who did that. It's lucky for Kaline that she's enveloped by sleep. The dog, in front as always, is already at the telescope. And looking very pleased. The powerful wagging of that tail! How he smiles. His smiling dog. How ludicrous, he thinks, watching dog hairs float in the air, towards the microscope. Although he loves his dog's friendly face, he shoos it out nonetheless. Then his eyes wander over his familiar instruments, the telescope, the electrostatic generator, to the wall where the magnets are hanging like hunting trophies once did in his father's forester's lodge. Oblong, oval, round, kidney-shaped and heart-shaped. Lined up beside each other they fill the space, no gaps. Which means they're all there, none is missing.

He takes a deep breath. Fetches a fresh doctor's coat from the cupboard, the pike-grey silk one as befits the occasion. With gold braid. And then white stockings. He exchanges the smoking jacket for fresh clothes and dabs some flower water on his brow. Takes from the wall two oval magnets and the heart-shaped one, brings them to the wooden table by the window, gives them a rub with a silk cloth.

It's been stormy and snowing all night. In the light of the courtyard lamp he can see that snow is still falling. Tiny, isolated flakes floating in the pool of light, as if they never wanted to touch the ground, but rather dance in the air forever. Like Mistress Ossine, whirled around by her anxieties like a snowflake in the wind.

She'll have had another diabolical night, no doubt. *I was lonely at night. And my loneliness let the devil in.* Those are her words. This is how Mistress Ossine articulates that she cannot speak better than she can think, and she cannot think better than her own grandmother.

But he, why has he got her flaky phrases dancing around in his head? It should be the other way round. His should be dancing around in her head. Nothing is as it should be on this early morning. Words from somewhere flash through his mind as if they were independent. He doesn't trust them. Words that seem to have no footing. Snatched from old, ancient air. Imprecise. Untrue. Words he has to translate in order to recognize himself.

When Mistress Ossine speaks of the devil it means she hasn't been able to sleep. She's been tossing and turning in her bed. Headache. Plus a hysterical fever. She's vomited and vomited till dawn.

All of which means she'll be calling for him every five minutes. In short, Mistress Ossine's diabolical night means Mesmer has a hellish day before him. Especially as the world consists of more than just Mistress Ossine. The new patient is called Maria Theresia. Her father, the court secretary, is a music lover. She herself is a virtuoso pianist. The family's well-known throughout the city. Even the empress knows her. And adores her. Maria Theresia. He will cure her. One thing follows another.

He places the magnets into the small bags lined with light-blue silk and pulls tight the drawstrings at the top. Two go into his doctor's bag, one into the inside pocket of his doctor's coat. He rearranges the material around his chest. He doesn't want anybody to notice anything. He doesn't want anybody to ask why he, the doctor, who treats sick people with magnets, is carrying a magnet next to his body. Is he ill himself, perhaps? A sick man trying to cure sick people? Highly suspect! He doesn't wish to have to explain anything. They're uneducated, they cannot understand him. Unlike his colleagues. They could understand. But they don't want to. Not Herr von Stuck-in-the-mud, and certainly not Dr

Ingenious. He didn't even want to understand when Mesmer cured Mistress Ossine before his very eyes.

A pig had broken out of its pen and galloped through the narrow alleyways of Vienna in a panic, almost colliding head on with Mistress Ossine. When they brought her to Mesmer she was unconscious. A good opportunity to demonstrate his abilities. He'd called for Ingenhousz to try to convince him that the magnetic principle was real. He didn't think that he would actually come and do exactly what Mesmer told him to, without question. But Ingenhousz chose one white china cup at random from six on the table and handed it to Mesmer so that the latter could transfer to it the magnetic power. Then Ingenhousz took all the cups to the unconscious girl in the room next-door. When she came into contact with the magnetic cup, her hand jerked back in pain. Ingenhousz repeated the experiment with all six cups. But the young girl only reacted to the magnetic one. Eventually she woke up and felt weak, but otherwise fine. Prof. Ingenhousz could scarcely believe it. Shook his head, said, incredible, saying it over and over again, as if he couldn't believe his own eyes. Until he admitted that he was convinced. Which meant that Mesmer was even more surprised when a few days later Ingenhousz made it known publicly that he had been witness to a fraudulent demonstration. A trick set up between Mesmer and a patient.

When Mistress Ossine, who was now walking with confidence again through the narrow alleyways of Vienna, learned that she'd been accused of setting up a hoax, her old convulsions returned. Mesmer had admitted her to his hospital.

Herr Dr Ingenious is not interested in healthy people. In

fact he can't abide them. He is attracted by the sick, with their bad and even worse symptoms, which he explains to them at great length. But what use are explanations? Isn't it enough to provide a cure? The Herr Dr is like all people. The flames of his vanity are easily fanned, but he is slow to warm to the truth. The truth is: a magnet gives power. Mesmer doesn't need to prove this. He can feel it.

Through the window he can see the cook crossing the courtyard. Perhaps it's later than he thought. His watch, where is his watch? He's going to be late. Kaline. Where's Kaline? The cook. No, asking the cook the time is like asking a raven for a piece of cheese.

The coachman is already waiting. For him. Out in the cold. He puts on his large black woollen coat, loops a thick woollen scarf around his neck. Dabs on some more rosewater, behind the ears this time, and carefully closes the door behind him. The dog greets him as if it hadn't seen him in days. It follows him outside. Once in the courtyard it goes its own way. Padding towards the stables, its paws in the fresh whiteness. Like black notes on white paper, Mesmer thinks. A melody enters his head. In the courtyard the snow muffles all sounds except for snow sounds. Mesmer's footsteps make such a loud crunch that he stops, alarmed, and looks up at his wife's bedroom. Upstairs, silence. What luck. Luck and silence, old bedfellows. But of course none of those ambitious types will take his word on this. They all assume that behind everything lies the incomprehensible. Which needs to be made comprehensible. He continues on tiptoe to the carriage. Into the splendid winter scene with two black horses in front of a sleigh. Two fully harnessed horses chew, turn their heads and then return to the oats in the sacks hanging by their mouths. The picture lacks a coachman. Other people are happy in their own company. But not him. He could embrace the horses, lean his head on their warm necks, stroke their croups. Horses do not drain power. On the contrary. They give power. But the new patient. And her father, the court secretary. An Imperial–Royal court secretary cannot do business with an unpunctual doctor or one who smells of horses.

All officials are the same. The more punctual and perfumed you are when you meet them, the more graciously they receive you. And what more could you wish for than to be received graciously? More graciously than graciously. Most graciously.

Hands in coat pockets, he gently walks on the spot. His right hand makes a major discovery: a watch on a chain. And when he pulls it out, there's no longer any hurry. And no sooner has the urgency vanished than everything goes like clockwork. The coachman hurries through the door of a neighbouring building, letting it slam shut behind him. Mesmer thinks this haste is mere pretence. After all, the coachman's sated expression suggests he has enjoyed a leisurely breakfast. And now, as he bids good morning to Mesmer, he takes the horses' breakfast away.

To the city centre, Mesmer says. He can drop him off at the Roter Turm. He'll walk from there to that house with the long name. What was it called? Schab den . . .

Zum Schab den Rüssel, the coachman says, cracking the whip until the horses get moving.

Usually the Danube catches the first rays of the morning

16

sun and takes hold of the last ones in the evening. Today, however, the snow has turned the Danube black. The Danube is a clock. It lets you tell the time, weather and season. He could organize his life by the Danube. By rivers in general, by bodies of water, by rising and falling tides. Which follow the movements of the planets. The constellations of the sun and moon. They influence the world. Everything we are made of, solid and liquid. He has studied the old writings, read Galileo, Gassendi, Kepler, Descartes. And he has studied nature, its wild gestures. The oceans – ebb and flow. The winds – gales and storms. The earth – quakes and volcanic eruptions. Mistress Ossine's seizures and twitches and countless other movements. Those of his wife, for example, with her irascibility and fits of anger. And his own – infrequent, thank God! – kidney pains. And soon, the body language of his new patient as well. He will study her blindness. And will turn a blind eye to the well-rehearsed routines. To the role being played out from memory. He will open the senses to her obduracy.

Amongst those men who he takes seriously, who like himself think scientifically and strive for precise measurements, many have suspected the influence of the universe on the world. But it was Newton who first arrived at universal principles. Clear head, clear language, clear laws. He's been studying Newton's system for years. It seems fairly certain that it makes sense. Newton is a great man. So great that he can even admit when he's at a loss. *I know there is an aether. I do not know what this aether is.* One of those phrases that make Newton inimitable. The phrase ticks in Mesmer's mind. Incessantly. Sometimes more quickly, sometimes more slowly

. . . Now, if permitted, a tiny remark . . . He has no wish to level any criticisms at him, but Newton, the physicist . . . is it at all possible that he perhaps just slightly underestimated the influence of the planets on all living things? Maybe just put slightly too much faith in his instruments? Mesmer is a physician. And physicians must delve further. Must pay serious attention to the smallest changes in the equilibrium. Even though these cannot be measured by new technology. What is a barometer against the moon? Which draws up the waters and air, accumulating them. So what if no measuring instrument has yet been able to calculate air tides. Does this mean they don't exist? Ridiculous. No, one has to delve further! Why can't they be measured? Because, of course, that wily fox the moon increases the weight of the air tides as it draws them up!

Bodies can feel where barometers fail. They are permeated by these tides. By the One. The Fluid. The most delicate substance, the most delicate of all substances in the universe. More delicate than the most delicate aether. That is law. His law. And let nobody contradict him. Especially not the gentlemen of the Academy. Especially not his former professor, his supervisor and witness, Anton von Störck! They will all have to acknowledge it. Peasants, priests, lawyers, doctors, musicians, music-lovers, cooks, coachmen, housemaids, the empress, her household, her ministers, her secretaries, her ladies-in-waiting and pages, her sons and daughters and all the young ladies in the land.

Vienna, the largest city in which he has ever lived. A large heap of stones. A stinking heap. Wherever you go it stinks, particularly in the scorching hot summers. Unbearable. And the people. So many of them that it would be impossible to know every single music-lover here. This city is swarming with music-lovers! It's swarming with musicians. They all want to come to Vienna, to the theatre, to the opera, to the court. And to the empress. She seems to be a magnet. A magnet with a force that can magnetize an entire city, a city as large as Vienna. And yet sometimes Vienna can be so tiny (and a hotbed of gossip) that you can find out everything about everyone easily. Sometimes more than you might wish. He's heard that the patient is in a sorry state. She's ugly. She is beautiful. In her suffering. She wears unflattering clothes. She plays piano better than she sings. She has a total cataract. She's just pretending to be blind. They only agree on one thing: the empress cherishes the girl beyond all measure, worships her even. He's going to cure her. He agrees with himself on this point. The rest is myth, he thinks, as the sleigh jolts to a halt.

Fresh snow all around. Scarcely a footprint to be seen. He calls out to the coachman to go on after all, and he looks out of the window as the horses trot slowly onwards. Until they arrive at a house with such monumental symmetry and so many windows that it looks as if it has eyes.

Slowly he walks up to the dark windows. And looks up to the second floor which is brightly lit. A blazing row of light which he stares into until the darkness vanishes from his eyes.

⤙ CHAPTER TWO ⤚

20 January, 1777
9.15 A.M.

❧⋆❧⋆

This is how people should be received. By a pretty, wide-awake housemaid, one who has been wide awake since the early hours. By the most natural housemaid in all Vienna, who casts you a brief glance at the door, a barely noticeable glance. And then who turns, waving her hand with a flourish, as if inviting you to dance, almost inviting misunderstanding. And then he follows this pale neck beneath pinned-up hair through the many dark corridors such as you would find in any house. Once in the drawing room it is light again, and she turns to him with a look that suggests he has now deserved her gaze, for a second at least. But she has stiff competition: a pianoforte. Not just one, but two pianofortes in the same drawing room. Mesmer can hardly avert his eyes from the instruments standing serenely side by side like the horses in front of the carriage with their open mouths.

He hears the girl's voice: Her master and mistress are ready for him right away.

And he, he thanks her for having shown him in. And when she lowers her eyes he says there's no hurry, please could she pass this on.

No sooner has the young girl left the room than he is sitting at the instrument.

He rests his right hand on his thigh and plays notes with his left. How rich they sound in this room, before blurring into one another. He notices how light the keys are. A Viennese mechanism, no doubt about it. The little Mozart would have enjoyed this. Would he have enjoyed his motif, too? G–B–E–D–A. A gentle flow. It pulls him along, will not let him go. He repeats it, varies the note lengths and rhythm, adds pauses and a trill. And meets the resonance of the notes with further notes. After a while he introduces his voice. Begins humming the changes before striking the notes on the piano.

A clearing of the throat from the door. The court secretary. Followed by his wife. A slim woman with a bonnet. And behind her, something indefinable.

The court secretary walks up to him. He says he can see he has the right man in the right house. It sounds pretty good. He knows how difficult it is to play the piano, from his own experience, of course. How many people can play the piano but also make it sound nice? He bows, and Mesmer endeavours to follow him as symmetrically as possible and at precisely the same time. Neither man should be able to watch the other while bowing.

Herr Paradis . . .

Herr von . . . , Paradis says.

No, not yet, Mesmer butts in, forcing the other man to repeat himself.

Herr von Paradis, he says.

He stood back up abruptly. And how stern he now sounds, the court secretary. Evidently his tone helps his wife enter the room, and the creature she has conjured up behind her turns out to be the daughter.

The first impression counts. It strikes him like lightning. With such force that he has to close his eyes momentarily. And then his head goes into a spin as he tries to filter the right, important things. Take it all in. The first view of the patient. The benchmark for everything to come, that must come, will have to come. No. He collects himself and his feelings. He will write it down. For fear of forgetting it.

The first impression: horrified when he sees her. And he's seen a lot in his time. And he knows enough to know that he's not squeamish. But nothing like this before.

Her closed eyes are in spasms. While the father, passing behind his wife as if straight through her, takes hold of his daughter and, his hand gripped tightly around her wrist, swings her once around in a semicircle.

She is pale, a wax figure made up with wax. Fitted out in her outfit. A doll. Now he can taste the doll's breath. But what? What was he was going to say? This dull, sweet taste in his mouth. The doll's powder on his tongue?

Her magnificent head of hair rises before him. A hair mountain. A powder ghost. An old hairpiece, towering above them all.

The girl is the tallest thing in the room. She is taller than the vase in the corner, which is almost as tall as a soldier. Taller than the stove. A monstrous child. With a décolleté. No, not a child.

He's heard, the court secretary says, that Mesmer had been making enquiries about his daughter. He was pleased that a doctor was asking after the invalid. Then he, the father, began making enquiries about the doctor. I was looking for you and you for my child.

He laughs, he doesn't say it, he laughs it.

Ribbons and bows are plaited into her locks. And little bells. Round and round like a procession.

Mesmer orbits her as if she were a planet. What's wrong? The planet has to orbit the star. And rotate while doing so. The star wants to see the sides. All of them. Even the darkest ones.

The father says he's solicited many different opinions about Mesmer, not all of them positive, he has to admit. But he wanted to make it clear that he was impartial. Convinced that Mesmer is a serious and scholarly man. And he's open to new methods. His new method. The magnets. When you've got a sick daughter you can't just listen to what people say. Can Mesmer imagine what you have to go through with a sick child?

Artificial trees are rooted in her hair, and stuffed birds sitting in tiny nests. Have they put real eggs under the birds? He imagines her parents might have done.

The dramatic drapery of her heavenly dress, the cracks in her powdery, dried-out make-up, the pale blue eggshells dotted in her hair. Just a representation of the truth in reality, he thinks. And all meant well, of course.

You will help her. The court secretary gives him the girl's wrist. It's limp and cold, like a smothered bird in Mesmer's hand.

The court secretary says he'd be happy to see any change in her, however small. Because anything is better than this. He points at her. He pushes her to the table.

The artificial locks on her head bob up and down animatedly. The girl herself seems to lack all elasticity. Every one of her movements seems as if it's being controlled externally. Her face like an abandoned nest, pressed flat, shaken and then pressed flat again. A mirror image of the hand he is still holding.

He'll be honest with him, he hears the court secretary say. He's already taken the child to a number of well-known doctors. Herr Dr Anton von Störck, who Mesmer already knows of course . . . and Dr Barth, the renowned cataract surgeon. Both declared her to be incurable. Mesmer and the girl both flinch when they hear the name. Now, as the father raises his voice, she twists her mouth.

No one has been able to help.

He's not surprised, Mesmer says, watching her head start to turn in his direction.

She's just as blind as she ever was, the father says.

The girl's mouth suddenly starts to quiver excitedly at the corners. Toying with a smile. What does it want? Does it want to detach itself from her face? Does it want to disappear?

And look, the father says, her eyes . . .

The secretary is still holding her arm. Mesmer her hand. He can feel the girl's hand starting to twitch.

As if her eyes were trying to burst out of their sockets, the father says. If it goes on like this, he says, they'll soon be rolling around my feet. Such a talent for music, and then this!

Such rotten luck. She's got it in her to make a professional career of it. Several lines, musical ones, are united in her blood.

My father, the mother states quietly, was a ballet master, court ballet master . . .

Please . . . , the court secretary says, putting his forefinger to his lips as a hint.

Blind or not . . . , he continues. Blind or not.

She wasn't always . . . , his wife tries again.

This time her husband raises his voice two levels at once.

His daughter has played in person for the empress. Played and sung. The occasion: a thanksgiving service for the victory at Planian in '57. In the Augustiner Barfüßer Hofkirche, the court church. He didn't have to mention her legendary *Stabat Mater*. Mesmer will have surely heard of it. Everybody's heard of it, the entire city. Everybody in Vienna, he adds, who loves her, the empress. And music. The empress, deeply moved. She'd granted Resi an honorary pension. Just imagine, he says, an honorary pension from the empress's own royal purse!

Not everybody gets that, Mesmer says.

Two hundred florins, for life, the father whispers. And with her help, he says, everything will be fine. Might he be able to say roughly how long they should expect . . . and the costs?

He couldn't say, Mesmer says. After all, he's barely seen the girl.

But she's sitting right here, the mother interrupts.

Does the doctor know, the mother says, that Resi only became blind when she was two? Overnight.

She should, the father snaps at her, let the doctor finish

what he was saying. Please, he says, speak, tell us what you wanted to say.

Mesmer says that he should like to find out more about that night.

There was an inexplicable commotion in the house. A nightmare, the court secretary says, the entire house. Including the staff, who have a tendency to dream. One single nightmare. Thieves and murderers. Thieves who became murderers. This is what they dreamed and screamed it out loud from their own dreams: thieves, murderers. Of course! Straw in the walls, straw in their heads! A nightmare. The screaming woke the house up. Everybody woke up. And drifted around in the dark in a panic. In the dark of the nightmare of the house.

The child, too, barely three years old. She had climbed out of her bed. And made her way unnoticed to the pitch-black floor immediately below.

Only discovered by the housekeeper hours later, sobbing quietly in the darkest corner.

She was brought back upstairs again. To her bed. This episode gave her a chill in her head. You know, he says, a draught. But it wasn't this house, they moved years ago. When he was appointed court secretary he was given this court accommodation. Now he was living here gratis, happily and well. More cheaply, more happily and better.

Even though the draught blew out the candles here as well, in Zum Schab den Rüssel – putting felt around the doors made little difference – compared with their old place, he says, it's dead still.

26

So the child had caught a chill in her head because of the draught?

Fear . . . , the mother says.

Fear, the father drowned her out, gave her the rest. The following morning she was blind.

Could he imagine such a terrible misfortune? the mother splutters. One's own child. The sweetest creature. The light of your life. That evening she's blinking at me with her beautiful, bright eyes. I kiss her, as I do every evening. And the next morning she's running into walls. As blind as a bat or a rat, as a . . . And she just stood there beside me, helpless. Could he imagine that? Surely he had children himself, and . . .

No, Mesmer says softly, my wife . . .

His wife, the father continues, hadn't given him a son either, regrettably. It wasn't her fault, of course. Just a daughter. She may have a talent, but that wasn't any help. It would have no effect on the continuation of his line, because in procreation it was the male seed which harboured everything that could be called talent and took root in the mother soil. So although his talent flourished in his daughter, alas it would end with her, too.

He's quite clearly one of the spermist faction, Mesmer says. But he should point out that the ovulist faction, that's to say those who believe that everything he calls talent is present in the female cell, is not made up exclusively of women. No, there were men, too. Men, and not only mummy's boys.

So what's the real truth? The court secretary is getting impatient.

They're still debating the subject.

27

I see, the court secretary says, avoiding the gaze of his irritated wife. Anyway, he adds, he's trying to make the best of the situation. It was a great shock for them all, not just for her, for all of them, for everybody who knows her.

Since then his wife has tried to be a set of eyes for her daughter. After all, it's the least she can do.

He'll make a note of Madame's sobbing. This hushed combination of groaning and snivelling. Like something that hurts and helps in equal measure. Like a deliverance that never quite reached its goal.

He's tried, the court secretary reflects, to make the best of the situation. It's the one thing he's been able to do. Making the best of the situation has always been his motto. Even back then, when he was stationed in the Banat, in the swamp. Where the climate's intolerable. Where he almost perished. Where, to survive, he had to make use of all his contacts. He pulled out all the stops to get away from there. And sought tutors for her, the best of course. The best tutors were the ones named by the best. Did Mesmer know how difficult it was to find a tutor for a blind girl?

Even educated people seemed to believe that someone who cannot see cannot understand either.

Yes, he could well imagine it, Mesmer says. It was down to the fact that people refuse to understand something that they cannot see . . . It made them blinder than blind . . .

He, the father said, had discovered that all this was complete nonsense. He'd read to his daughter, as often as possible, didn't I, Resi?

The girl nods.

Read to her over and over again. Nothing that might have corrupted her heart, nothing of course that might have reduced further her utility as a woman, seeing as how limited this was by her illness anyway. We only read useful things. God and Gellert were our favourites, weren't they, Resi.

Come on, he says, give us a little snippet, Resi.

And Resi, with the gently swaying tower of a head, murmurs,

> *Dear little hourglass, please go quick,*
> *Make the sand run out in a tick,*
> *Let the sand run,*
> *Let it be One,*
> *Dear little hourglass, please go quick.*

Well, Resi, now you're surprising me. This is new. He'd never heard that before. She's made it up herself. You never know with Resi's talent, the father says. There's only one thing that's patently clear: you don't need eyes for everything. She can think and speak quite happily without them. Quite apart from playing piano. His daughter has also taught him that you can see many things better without eyes. Go on, Resi, tell us what the falcon in Gellert's fable looks like.

He's blue. And he's got yellow dots on his eyes.

Wrong . . . the mother says. That's . . .

That's the parrot, the father says.

The falcon, you know, the one from . . .

Leave her in peace, the father says. Don't worry, Resi.

Beneath her lids he can see her eyes circle like two baby birds just before hatching.

I think the child's had enough, the father says. She should sleep.

Did she still have a vivid recollection of that night? Mesmer asks her directly.

She knows the story, the father says, but she can't remember anything.

Really? Mesmer says. You don't remember anything at all?

No, the father says.

What is your earliest recollection, Fräulein?

There is no earliest, the father says, thank God. Now she just remembers the good things, don't you Resi? Do you remember playing for the empress?

The daugher's closed eyes turn towards the mother. The bright bells of her magnificent hair accompany each movement. Mesmer listens.

Go on, tell us what the empress shouted out, the mother says.

The girl nods eagerly.

Yes. Bravo. She shouted Bravo, the court secretary answers his wife.

And then, Mesmer says, what happened then?

The girl claps her hands.

Exactly, the father says, the honorary pension!

And then? Mesmer says.

That's it, the father says.

Might it be possible to hear it from her, Mesmer says.

The mother laughs out loud. The court secretary puts a finger to his lips. They all wait.

The girl's face twitches, gently at first, like a storm brewing

30

behind her eyelashes. Then her eyes open slowly.

They open wide, bulge out. The pupils leap around uncontrollably, like balls bouncing down stairs. Or like boats which are too small for waves which are too big, or like fish lunging at specks of dust they think are gnats, or like the first flies of the spring around bunches of dried flowers. Everything which was just dead, lifeless, now flies into turmoil, twitching, vibrating according to its own system, independent of the whole. Chaotic and uncoordinated like an automaton gone mad.

Close your eyes! the father shouts.

The girl obeys. She switches off.

What a sight. The father strives to maintain his composure.

It's good, the mother says softly, that the doctor has seen it.

There's no need for you to speak, the father says. She should play for the doctor instead. What are you going to play for us, Resi?

The girl stands, finds her way to the piano and stretches her back. How effortlessly she speaks!

I'm going to play a piece by my teacher. My most revered Meister Koželuh. A short piece, his own composition.

She raises her hands which metamorphose in mid-air, turning into soft clouds that nestle as light as a feather on the keys.

As soon as the first notes ring out Mesmer takes a deep breath.

Bravo, he shouts when she finishes. Does she know anything by Gluck?

The girl shakes her head.

Gluck, no, the father says. Salieri. But that's enough now. Can Mesmer help?

He will bring her eyes under control, Mesmer says. Soothe and encourage them back into their sockets.

Sounds like a good start, the father says. And it should be worth Mesmer's while.

Mesmer gives him an enquiring look.

Well, the father says more quietly. This proximity to the very top . . . perhaps the empress herself might take an interest in the case . . . if she were to hear of it . . . and they might, possibly, be able to be of assistance . . . Did he understand?

Yes.

So what would happen then with her eyes?

He didn't like to speculate, Mesmer says. He would rather get going immediately than offer big promises. The theory was important, but this was not what changed things. It was the practice which showed how valuable a theory was. Not the other way around.

Now he asks the parents to leave the room. He needs some time with the patient.

Alone? the mother says.

Of course, the father says, his wife will leave the room. He waves her over to the door.

Mesmer looks from one to the other in disbelief.

He'll be happy, the father says, to sit in a corner. Just pretend I'm not here.

Mesmer shakes his head.

But look. The father points to the girl. Look how her body's trembling again. Dancing like a puppet on strings, on strings outside in the storm, and all alone.

Very nicely put! Mesmer says, and anyway her trembling is a good sign. And this is why he suggests that the girl should come and stay in his magnetic hospital.

Was he not overstating things somewhat now?

No, on the contrary, he was far from overstating things.

They'd come to an agreement with Herr von Störck and Herr Barth. She'd gone to them for treatment twice a week.

He couldn't be compared to these gentlemen, Mesmer says, and nor was his method anything like theirs.

My daughter does not leave this house just like that, the father says.

The pianoforte. She needs the piano. Her daily practice is like breathing to her. Surely he knows, her professional career . . .

He, too, Mesmer says, believes that idleness is the beginning of every illness. So it's particularly fortunate that there's a piano at his house, entirely at her, the daughter's, disposal. And to be more specific, he says, it's one with an English mechanism. The action just a touch heavier. Perfect for strengthening tender hands and fingers. It's only tiring if you haven't practised enough. Soon you can play it in your sleep, and it sounds like a dream.

⤙ CHAPTER THREE ⤚

21 January, 1777

He had hardly slept. He was scribbling notes until late into the night. Reading through them over and over again. Wondering whether the notes might not interpose themselves between himself and the girl. And how much of what he's jotted down, out of fear of forgetting it, has actually got something to do with the girl.

Until his wife called him and he pretended not to hear. Even though he was usually happy to obey her calls. But right now one final thought was pressing for one final note. Until Anna, in nightdress and bonnet, stood behind him, a candle in her left hand and a candle in her right, and he was terrified that if he continued to ignore her she would fly off into one of her rages. He hadn't heard anything. Was going through his notes for his latest case. Yes, a partial success already, from tomorrow Fräulein Paradis would be his patient. Anna congratulated him, she wanted him to tell her all about the famous blind girl, and all his plans for her. She wanted to be in on this case from the start. She'd already learned so much from him, and still had plenty to learn. The method he talked about. She was pleased.

He got up, left the notes on his desk, and followed her up the stairs. She wanted to talk more about his new case. He was happy to be able to lie down next to her in bed. And she squeezed his head between her hands and gave him a lengthy kiss on the mouth until he started kissing her back and pushed up her nightdress. The sounds she emitted. Like the sounds of tiny industrious animals, he thought, who don't need to know what they're doing. Focusing totally on the job. So absorbed in each other that they start screaming. When she started screaming he stroked her mouth, tracing the shadow of her lips, and put his hand over it to hold himself back. She opened her eyes, only briefly, and went silent. He wasn't expecting that. Rather the opposite. He liked her voice. And was missing it already.

The voice provides information about a person, he thought. It's their key, their colour. A person's voice allows you to guess where, in which climactic region they are at home. In the cold, such as the Greenlanders who have converted to the cross; or in the heat, such as the Rapa Nui of the Easter Islands who have converted to the cross; and his wife.

Anna had fallen asleep long ago, but he was still thinking about voices.

About one in particular, one which he couldn't recall because she had scarcely said a word: the voice of his new patient. The father was the girl's voice here. He wondered whether she spoke more when she was alone with her parents. He wanted to hear her voice before he began the treatment. He was kept awake wondering how he should arrange this. Then the patient bell rang, at this early hour. He could tell who it was by the ring. Only Mistress Ossine rang for so long and so insistently. (And only since she had started telling him about her former life. In which headaches had been almost totally absent.)

It was just after four. He found her distraught in her ruffled bed, her fist hammering against her head.

She couldn't bear the pain, she said. In the night the devil had bored his horns into her eyes. Here, right through her head. As she said this her upper body went into a spasm and she threw up at his feet. It spattered. He took a step backwards.

He gave her a cloth which she used to pat her mouth clean. He said he would fetch a magnet. Then he held her hand and placed his other one on her head. Immediately she said she felt better. And now he mustn't leave her alone. She was always alone. Which was when the devil laid his hands on her. Barely twenty heartbeats later she was asleep and didn't notice Mesmer, together with his hand, skulking away from her. He hadn't fetched the magnet. It hadn't been necessary. He didn't understand why, but so much the better.

He didn't go back to bed. Didn't go to his laboratory. Waiting meant filling the time with thoughts of what he could have done. He wished it weren't so early in the morning or that Messerschmidt weren't such a night owl. And that he could just fly there: to Messerschmidt's workshop in the Landstraße, which was not terribly far away. Take a look at his new sculptures. Everyone's appalled by them. Give his friend some encouragement and tell him he shouldn't feel browbeaten. And let himself be encouraged in turn. Convince him to stay. As they drink freshly brewed black coffee. The Viennese aren't that bad. You just shouldn't take them as seriously as they do themselves.

Until he heard Kaline's familiar noises. The tongs banging against the stove, the cinders being scraped out and brushed into a pot. When he came face to face with Kaline these sounds seemed to him too fierce. He bade her good morning and instructed her to clean Mistress Ossine's room. She needed rest and would not be taking part in the baquet today. Kaline should see to this.

Understood, Kaline said in disgust. But it was far too early for that sort of thing. First she had to light the fires and lamps, and then make breakfast. Or did he want to plunge the house into chaos?

She wouldn't dare speak to his wife like that. She knows my wife wouldn't let her get away with that, he thought. And said: Of course he didn't want any chaos. With a blanket around his shoulders he returned to the treatment room.

He flipped up the lid of the magnetic baquet. He checked the water level in the vessel, added some water and iron filings, arranged the bottles at the base of the baquet in a star formation, and shut the lid again. He took out the metal rods hanging askew in their holders, carefully replacing them so they now hung straight. Too early to play music, too late to go back to sleep. He wanted at least to make use of the morning peace. The dog joined him on the way to his laboratory. It looked again as if it was laughing. Which should not come as a surprise. It never let anybody or anything rob it of sleep. I envy those who can manage that, he thought. He would have loved to have taken a sample of his dog's saliva and examined it under the microscope. But there was insufficient light. He would have loved to have seen those tiny organisms which he had already discovered in such large numbers in all possible liquids and bodily fluids, in his own blood first of all. Which swam around so dangerously happy, as if they were utterly at peace with the world. And he had tried to find the sperm worms described by Leeuwenhoeck. The children already formed in them. Without success. Others had found more. All he had seen in his was that something was moving around. Was that down to the quality of his microscope or the quality of his seed? Or was his observation faulty? He would like to know more precisely. Whether his sperm might be judged sufficiently good for reproduction.

If Mistress Ossine knew how little alone we actually are, he thought.

Microscopic experiments thrilled him almost as much as playing music. Except: after playing he felt relaxed. As after an extended sleep. It was gradually getting light. He washed, put on his purple silk doctor's coat and purple trousers. And snow-white tights of course. When dawn broke the purple really started gleaming. A royal colour. Whenever he saw the morning appear like this he felt as if he were coming down to earth from a great height. The lighter it became, the more earthly he felt.

Shortly after ten Kaline knocked.

She had done everything he'd asked.

Why was she telling him this? Was she trying to appease him? He didn't understand her. He was never sure whether her behaviour was terribly polite or precisely the opposite (something which was not provable). But, he reflected, wasn't it the real duty of science to prove the existence of the opposite of the provable?

Some patients from outside had already arrived, she said. They were sitting with the residents at the health baquet. Mistress Ossine, moreover, had refused to stay away. In fact she'd been the first one in the room. Even before the musicians.

At that moment he can hear Riedinger tuning his violin.

To get rid of her he asks Kaline to let the dog out.

He closes his eyes. A Haydn adagio is playing. Everything splendid. Hossitzky joins in with his horn.

When the dog barks Mesmer opens his eyes. He can see the Paradis's coach passing in front of his laboratory window. Stopping in the middle of the courtyard. The dog, barking and wagging its tail, trots over to the carriage,

He sees the court secretary jump out of the carriage and avoid the dog's greeting. Putting his hands up to its muzzle. He sees the court secretary's feet slip and then recover. Only just.

He shouts something. Is he cursing? Or warning his wife? It's slippery.

Now the secretary's wife gets out of the carriage and helps her child down. She holds a hand over her daughter's hair in protection.

The three of them, the tall child in the centre, approach the house. The girl visibly smaller than yesterday, and yet . . . Still taller than her parents. The dog swaggers in front of them.

The doorbell. He waits. Why is nobody opening? It rings again. Where is Kaline?

By the time he runs off his wife has opened the door and is showing them into the drawing room. Why is she up already?

He stands by the door to the drawing room. Listens to his wife's impeccable politeness. It doesn't fool him. Her tone contradicts her words.

She invites the three of them to take a seat. Her voice is quivering. She leaves the room, boiling with anger.

Has he seen Kaline? That bitch! This really is the last time. Whenever you need her she vanishes into thin air. On principle.

She's right, he says, he thinks that, too. Even though he doubts whether Kaline has any principles. She's like most of them: a pent-up creature always colliding with the present and making sparks fly.

He utters phrases to placate his wife. The feeling that she's always on fire. His wife, a dormant volcano, which could erupt at any moment. And he, a daily drop of dew on the steep, sprawling slope. Mesmer has prescribed the volcano an infusion of hop blossoms and valerian root, three times a day.

Anna leaves him standing there. Races off to find Kaline. Mesmer knows that when he enters the drawing room the girl will be as silent as yesterday.

He exploits the opportunity, listens at the door. Is she talking to her parents? What is she saying?

There are doctors who gauge the severity of an illness by pouring a drop of oil into the patient's urine. If the oil swims at the top, the patient will soon get better. If the oil stays in the middle, it is going to be a long illness. If it sinks to the bottom, they are at death's door. Mesmer prefers to let the tone of the voice tell him what's wrong with the patient. Why does he have such well-trained hearing? And he sees the voice as that part of the tree which grows above the ground, its roots being the nerve pathways which branch through the entire body. And, after all, this is his business. Nerves and the nervous system.

Who is able to sit still in an unfamiliar house? The court secretary wanders around, knocking the walls. He praises the solid construction.

A doctor's the thing to be, he hears the wife say. Her voice risen to admiration. Look at the bust, she says. That must be the doctor himself. Looks like him, doesn't it?

Except the bust seems to have fewer worries, the court secretary laughs. Or can you see any wrinkles? There's a draught in here, he says all of a sudden. Resi, can you feel the draught?

Now. Mesmer holds his breath. Waits.

Nothing. Silence. The young lady says nothing.

Maybe she's shaking or nodding her head. He bets she's nodding, and that the parents are gazing at the curtain. The red velvet curtain that hides all sorts of things behind it, but definitely not all draughts.

The court secretary's wife is speaking.

Yes, there is a draught in here. But it's nowhere near as bad as in Schab den Rüssel. Maybe he could give us some advice . . . she's very willing to learn about air movements.

Well, he's happy that *he's* not a doctor! The court secretary sounds gruff. After all, in his position you get to shake the hand of the most interesting people of the day. The geniuses of our age, he says. Think of Salieri, he says. Such a renowned musician and composer. And our Resi's taking singing lessons from him! Not bad, eh, Resi?

Mesmer presses his burning ear against the cold wood of the door. No answer is an answer too. The court secretary is swooning. Hofrat von Kempelen! He's done so many good things for our daughter! Just think, such a great man teaching our daughter to read. With letter boards that I didn't even know existed, what about you?

Me? the mother says. No, how could I? I'm a woman.

Pestalozzi's great letter boards! And now he's building an automaton that can play chess. Just imagine, he says, an automaton that can speak. A sensation! No one else would ever think of that. I mean, would you have ever thought of an automaton that can speak?

Me? she says. Never.

And not just that, he says. He's also developing a writing machine for blind people. Just imagine! Our Resi will be able to write independently. And Metastasio. The poet, the greatest in the whole Monarchy. But above all of these, way above them, of course, the empress herself.

The wife sighs. Not a sound from the daughter.

This is such a magnificent house. When she sees this magnificent house, she says, she feels bad that Resi hasn't come with an appropriate hairstyle. It's only because the tall, formal hairpiece from Paris doesn't fit in the carriage. Why don't they make carriages bigger? Why should generations of women have to duck their heads or go around with hair like crushed profiteroles? Has anybody really understood what that means? People ought to think of things like this. These crazy inventions are all very well and good. But sometimes it's the things closest to you which are the most important . . . And a person's hairstyle is not their least significant aspect. It is on top of the head after all. Where reason resides, as he's fond of saying.

Yes, but, the court secretary says. Not everybody has reason residing there. Once again she's being vague in her wording.

She starts by talking about women and then, just now, she says people. Who does she really mean? At most women account for half of all human beings, she needs to be more specific, he says.

In any case, there was no consensus as to whether women belonged to the same species; from what he'd heard the debate on this matter in educated circles had not yet reached a satisfactory conclusion.

He, a man without a son, a man equally blessed and afflicted by having a wife and daughter, he of course, well naturally he had to believe that . . .

A short pause follows and Mesmer is about to open the door. But when the mother starts talking to the daughter he decides to wait.

Don't worry, Resi, she says, even if your hair is not quite so neat today, it's neat enough. The hairpiece might not be from Paris, but it is brand new. Made only recently by the Imperial–Royal wigmaker. With fresh hair from the Frankfurt Hair Fair; it's well known that this is the best hair to be had for far and wide. Freshly collected from all the battlefields of the empire . . . And at the top, the bonnet, *à la Matignon*, that really was from Paris, the city of cities, and it made up for everything.

And Resi, she adds, just so you know where you are: apart from this splendid bust of the doctor beside the stove, where he looks like a young god, there's also a huge mirror hanging on the wall. I'm looking at you in it now, from behind, in your sweet dress, it's a lovely sight! And next to it there are three pictures in ornate frames. One of them is of Dr Mesmer, another of his elegant wife . . . who just let us in.

Surely that's his mother! the court secretary interrupts.

And the third one . . . in the middle, she continues, their son.

The doctor hasn't got a son, the father says. His wife's made a mistake.

So who does he think the boy is?

Resi, he turns to his daughter. The doctor hasn't spoken of a son, has he?

Now Mesmer puts his ear to the door again and holds his breath. For a long time. They're all waiting. Is she trying to remember? Now. She's talking, she's talking! And the first thing she says is: his name.

Mesmer, she says.

Her voice sounds gentle. Weak and soft and delicate. It flows without any power, but it flows. And is alert. And tuneful. When she speaks her voice does not sound gravely ill. Her voice is a drop of oil swimming at the surface, no, floating above it. Excellent prognosis. And she's saying more.

Mesmer, she says, didn't speak of a son. But if someone doesn't mention a son, it doesn't mean there isn't one.

He calls that a logical statement. Mesmer hears the court secretary slapping his thigh. Excellent, my child. What a brilliant son you would have made!

Mesmer thinks her voice sounds muffled, as if it were swaddled in wool. Swaddled in something, anyway. Something wrapped up. Packed up by her parents. Like a cake on a journey . . . he notes. Not the cake, but the fact that it's packed. And he's full of confidence. That he will unpack her. Make her flow. He can see it, hear it, taste it even.

Look! The wife sounds surprised. The bust is by the same artist who portrayed the empress. She recognizes the initials: F.X.M.

Mesmer is about to open the door, but stops when the voice of the court secretary suddenly explodes.

He's not waiting any longer. He was not appointed secretary to the Imperial Department of Commerce so he could hang around waiting for people. If the quack didn't come immediately he'd get straight back in his carriage.

And his wife: Did he not wish to do something for someone else, just for once?

Whoever did anything for him? Anyway he had more important things . . .

Mesmer waits for a moment, then regains his composure and yanks open the door.

That's him, the court secretary says angrily. About time too. He doesn't want to leave his daughter here guessing. He wants to see the magnets. Finally wants to find out something about the new method.

His heart sinks. As soon as Mesmer has to explain what he is doing, people misunderstand him.

He's not fond of explanations. He'll give a short demonstration instead. To answer all the questions they may still have.

Very good. The court secretary smiles. The girl starts to tremble and clutches her mother's arm. Don't worry, Resi. The mother frees her fingers one by one, and one by one they clutch on tight again.

Mesmer takes a long black cane from behind the curtain and stands beside the girl.

Here is my hand, he says, placing it on her arm.

At that moment the mother succeeds in freeing herself. The girl lets herself be taken three paces to a chair.

A place from where Mesmer has a good view of her in the mirror. Mesmer asks her to sit.

His hand moves up from her arm to her neck. Stays there. With the other he holds and raises the Spanish cane, aiming it at the young lady's reflection. Very slowly, he moves it from right to left.

The court secretary and his wife watch their daughter as if spellbound. The girl slowly moves her head this way and that. As soon as Mesmer waves the cane in a circle, her head moves in a circle, too.

The wife screams in fright, tugging at her husband's arm and pointing out the synchronous movements.

Very interesting, the court secretary says. Really strange.

46

He's not seen anything like that, ever. Can she see it too? he says to his wife.

She can see it because he can see it. Otherwise she'd never believe it.

That's not the point, he says, whether you believe it or not. The fact is, he's seeing what he's seeing. And even if what he's seeing is impossible, he's got to believe it.

They follow Mesmer to the patients' wing. For the sake of the patients who are sitting in the health baquet, he has requested they be silent. But they cannot keep from whispering, the court secretary and his wife. The daughter still between the two of them. They don't stop. To Mesmer they seem like the geese in the shed outside, who feel themselves, each other and everything else with their beaks.

In the treatment room Riedinger and Hossitzky are playing the last movement of the Haydn sonata. Mesmer stands beside them. The patients sway to the sounds of the violin and horn as if they were a single organism moving underwater. What use are words, explanations? What good would it do if he said they were linked up to a magnetic Fluid? That it was flowing right through them? The beneficial Fluid came through the rods and ropes and was also passed on from one person to another. And the music intensified the flow even further. Different from words. Words stir words. And nothing else. Momentum cannot be proven by words. Nothing can be proven. Not by words, nor phrases, treatises.

Resi, he hears the wife whisper, it's pretty dark in here. We probably won't see much more than you.

47

But enough to make out a group of ill men and women. And there's a small boy sitting between them.

They're all sitting around a wooden vessel, she explains. With a wooden lid. In front of each patient is an opening in the lid, and sticking through these are metal rods that can be pulled out because they're attached to ropes. The upper halves of the rods are bent at right angles.

The small boy's pointing the rod at the side of his head, she whispers. And I can see a woman, a very sick woman. Much sicker than you. She's completely slumped. If the rod wasn't supporting her head she'd tip over. She's also put the rope around her neck as if she were on the gallows. And her eyes are closed.

All of them have their eyes closed, not just her, the court secretary interrupts. And they're all holding hands, he continues. Just as you like doing, Resi. And, Resi, he says, you know how much I hate infirmaries. I can't abide them. They're intolerable.

But here, with this nice music, he doesn't feel unwell yet. A good sign, Resi, he says.

Not just good, his wife says, it's impressive, seeing these people doze in a room of purple velvet. And all those mirrors everywhere. Mightily impressive. Even the doctor dressed in matching colours. If only you knew what colours were. Colours are so . . . so tasteful. Like everything in this house, she says, glancing at Mesmer.

A loud sighing from one of the patients silences her. Somebody is breathing noisily, the deepness and rapidity increase. Mesmer, who has an inkling of what's about to happen, gives the musicians a sign. As if a valve had been opened, Mistress Ossine starts to scream. Fräulein Paradis winces, crumples up, opens wide her bulging eyes, while Ossine screams and screams and stretches up high, as rigid as a plank.

Riedinger and Hossitzky know what to do. They drop their instruments, remove the ropes, and carry the rigid, screaming young woman from the room. Mesmer notices Fräulein Paradis's entire body start to convulse. She's sensitive. Unbelievably sensitive. Mesmer, who would have loved to study her sensitivity, runs to the door, passing close to the girl whose right arm is fastened tight around her mother. The court secretary has grabbed her left arm and is shaking it. The parents are whispering to their daughter. In vain.

The woman who's screaming has just had a bad dream, Resi. It's all fine. They picked her up, the wife shouts, and carried her out of the room. So the poor wretch can calm down. The doctor's hurrying to her now. It's all fine, the parents say, their voices trembling. And their knees.

Mistress Ossine chooses the worst possible moments for her crises.

It worked. Ossine's sleeping. In the crisis room where they took her. On the mattress. Mesmer has tied magnets to her feet. And one each on her stomach and chest. To begin with she was screaming even louder, but then she quietened down and started groaning. He thought he would soon be able to return to the treatment room. But the groaning dragged on. And he was not focused. Was thinking of the young girl. Then he did something he had never done to a patient before: he put his hand over her mouth. He did it with the intention of curtailing the crisis. He shouldn't have done. A crisis is a crisis. And every patient has a right to their crisis. And he the duty to stand by her. But he was only thinking of the new patient. And had gently placed his hand on Ossine's lips. With instant effect. Instead of coming to, she groaned more loudly. Shifted about under his hand and started snatching at his fingers, licking his hand, as if she were no more than a large, wet mouth to which he had to attend. He let her have his hand. It wasn't pleasant. And yet he is captivated by all life. She started sucking his fingers. It lasted until she opened her eyes and talked to his hand. It's fine now. She can feel it. Please, let her have his hand.

When she'd gone to sleep he went in search of the Paradis family.

He found them in the piano room. Where the parents turned their heads towards him. The mother full of reproach, the father more resentful. Both are still wearing expressions of horror. Their daughter at the piano is racing through scales, up and down the keyboard. She chases through every key as if she were trying to leave something behind, as if her fingers were speeding away from something. Nobody has played that quickly on this piano since it was ravaged by the young Mozart. Dizzyingly fast. And with such powerful resonance.

Resi's trying out the instrument, the court secretary says, its action, the sound, the mechanism. After the final C sharp she begins a slow piece that Mesmer doesn't recognize.

Her own composition, the mother whispers.

He didn't know that she composed, Mesmer whispers back. But it makes sense. Where the female aspect cannot be fulfilled by a male one – and the young lady is hardly heading for a man – the creative activity of composing fully compensates for this male aspect.

The mother looks at her husband.

She doesn't understand what the doctor has just said.

It's quite simple, the court secretary whispers. He said that Resi will never marry. And so she should happily go on composing.

At that moment the young girl lifts her hands from the keys, nods and says, yes, that will be fine, she's happy with the piano, they've become friends.

What on earth was wrong with that woman all of a sudden? the court secretary wants to know. Her behaviour was insufferable.

The patient had a *crisis*.

What sort of illness is that, a *crisis*? Is it infectious?

Not an illness at all. Rather something akin to the mode of an illness, if he understood what he meant.

The mode of an illness. Aha, the father laughs wearily. As he always does when he fails to understand. He knows the word mode from music. So the illness changes from major to minor? Well, he'd have to . . .

Think, Mesmer says, about the character of a piece of music. A *crisis*, he says, hesitating, most resembles a presto. But unlike in music, where a presto is not that much more than an adagio, a *crisis* is a sort of climax of all types of illness.

Afterwards an illness gets weaker. Health gets stronger. *Vous comprenez?*

Right, the court secretary says, so a *crisis* is something to be welcomed. The climax but also the beginning of the end. Do you understand, Resi? he says.

The girl nods and lowers her head.

You could put it like that, Mesmer says.

But he wanted to know how this woman was now. Whether she'd come round yet. In plain language: *Je voudrais jeter un coup d'œil dans la chambre.* He'd like to take a brief glance in the room next door, the court secretary says.

Mesmer is sorry. Out of the question. After a crisis the patient needs total rest.

If he's going to allow his little girl to be left here for the next few weeks, the secretary says, he needs to know what's going on.

The court secretary is sticking to his guns.

She's never been away from home for so long before.

Now, Mesmer says abruptly, he'll show them the room she'll be staying in, then he'll have to bring this audience to an end. His patients are calling for him.

Don't go, the girl says, when the parents take their leave. She clings to her mother. Your hands . . . she says softly when her mother frees herself from her. The court secretary hustles his wife towards the carriage.

Bye-bye, Resi. And be happy. Soon you won't have to grab onto everything with such urgency.

He waves to her.

And Mesmer looks at the dog, which is sitting upright by the door. Its back stretched, ears pointed, it watches the two of them leave. As if their departure was no less exciting than their arrival.

⤜ CHAPTER FOUR ⤛

24 January, 1777

⤜⤛⤜⤛

Anybody who comes early will find him at his glass armonica. When Kaline opens the door he's playing a piece by Gluck. It's upsetting to have to interrupt a piece. He plays on and, without wishing to, notices everything that comes through the door in Kaline's wake.

A puffed-up dress, a towering coiffure and a black dog. His dog.

The thought that Kaline isn't doing her job properly is interfering with his playing. Kaline ought not to have let her wear this. Should have had a word. From one woman to another. Not the ball gown when seeing the doctor, please. This is going to cost him an hour, all those ribbons, the ruches, tresses.

When the dog nudges him with its nose, he capitulates. Breaks off from playing, strokes the dog's head, nods enquiringly at Kaline and watches her flounce out of the room with a shrug. He greets the young woman.

She's sitting upright, her hands folded across her chest like something closed, no, something barricaded behind itself. Like something to which you can say whatever you want, but nothing gets through. He tries, all the same. A phrase which is a tried and tested opening line.

Would she tell him a little about herself?

Nothing.

When the dog goes over to her, prodding her with its muzzle, she takes her hand away.

Doesn't she like the dog?

No, she says.

Why not?

She doesn't like any dogs.

But this isn't just any dog, he says.

It's the offspring of a particularly smart dog. Once, when Mesmer had just finished running an errand at the pharmacy on Neuer Markt, the dog's smart father appeared out of the blue and stuck to his heels. To start with he thought the dog had mistaken him. He looked around for the owner. Asked people who the dog belonged to. Nobody recognized it. Nobody had ever seen it. He tried to shoo the dog away. In vain. The dog would not be shooed away. When, later on, he got into his carriage to return here, the dog had run behind the carriage and arrived at the same time as him.

An old mongrel, she says. That's what they call vile things like that in her family.

He didn't let it come into the house, Mesmer continues. At least not for a week. Gave it nothing to eat. But still the dog stayed. It was a black dog. Just like this one, its son. Jet-black.

He gradually got used to the dog. This good-natured animal was continually trying to please him. Following him around like a well-meaning shadow. It couldn't be lured away with any of the tasty morsels his wife offered up. The only thing it couldn't bear were rooms where all the doors were closed. At night it stayed outside in front of the house, even if it was cold or wet. Of course, nobody noticed that it soon became attached to a female dog that nobody had ever noticed either: the coachman's dog. That's what happens with things that nobody notices. They bear the most noticeable fruit. Not straight away. At some point, as if out of the blue. On another occasion when I went to the pharmacy, the dog was with me as ever. After making my purchases, I paid a visit to the small tavern in Kärntnerstraße to ask the porter in the rear courtyard about an address. It was then that I saw a stranger looking down from a window into the courtyard.

He calls out something, a name. And like a bullet the dog shoots into the house and up the stairs to the stranger. The dog, brimming with joy, almost performed a somersault. The fact that it had heeded the stranger's call left no room for doubt. This man was its real master. Indeed, he told Mesmer he'd reared the dog in Russia, Moscow to be precise, and lost him there ten months ago.

But, the girl says, why did the animal pick you out when it arrived in Vienna? Why did it follow you everywhere as if it were stuck to you? And why should it refuse to enter closed rooms? Are you saying it felt, or suspected that it would end up in Vienna, where on a particular day this man would take it to a place where its real master would be gazing out of a courtyard window? That it suspected this was the only way of being reunited with its former master. And why outside the whole time? For fear of being shut in at the crucial moment?

She's asking exactly the right questions, Mesmer says. And exactly those that he asks himself.

She, the girl says, thinks it rather improbable. How on earth could the dog have known all that?

That's the key question, Mesmer says. He waits a while, then asks whether she'd like to tell him about herself now.

She says nothing.

He knows from other patients that they don't just sit there, thinking nothing at all. They often look as if they couldn't move another muscle, but inside their minds are whizzing around.

⚔ CHAPTER FIVE ⚔

24 January, 1777
12.15 p.m.

※～※～

She lowered her eyes. What should she tell him about? Yesterday? Today? Now? Herself? What does he mean?

Everything enters her mind. Everything at once. So nothing. Nothing but fragments. The instrument he was playing is still ringing in her ear. Those notes. Which flew away before they had properly settled. Blended into each other. As if each note were too large for a single pitch. As if several chords were flowing out of the note and in all directions. A fading polyphony. Almost sad. Sadly excited. Once, her most esteemed namesake spoke about the abandoned, decaying gardens of the Villa d'Este. About the channels of the River Teverone. About the harmony of the water that flowed and cascaded in all directions. And about how this had once been set to music by the architect Galvani, who surely would have made a first-rate composer, too. She liked that. And the fact that the empress wants to bring the whole thing back to life. This fading polyphony.

She could say that she doesn't know what the last note he

actually played was. But the doctor might then question her hearing. And her hearing is extraordinarily good. She is proud of her hearing. She would rather talk about last night. She hardly slept a wink. The strange bed. Strange creaking of strange floorboards. Strange footsteps outside her room. Even her own, familiar footsteps sound strange in the unfamiliar room. Seven paces from one wall to the other, and five from the window to the bed. A spacious room. And the walls smooth and cold. And early in the morning a dog, barking at the dawn as if it were a stranger, too. At least there's another awake apart from her, even if it's only an animal.

The jet-black dog, as the girl said. But she's getting ahead of herself again, leaving out the most important things.

The strange hand which shook awake the insomniac. She recognizes people by their hands. Cool, dry, moist, warm, soft, padded, uptight, gouty, rough, bony, wiry, fat, coarse, relaxed. Should she say that she doesn't like all hands? Only the soft ones. They feel like bright voices, resonating with themselves. Such as the one which said it was Kaline, the housemaid. Did she wish to get up and have breakfast? And which, almost without waiting for an answer, asked further questions: Gruel? Roasted bread? With preserved plums and apricots from the garden? She sounds so natural, this Kaline. Touches her shoulder so naturally. And can tell naturally from her sleepy mouth what she wants, when she suggests: How about a nice big cup of hot chocolate?

Kaline brings her clothes to the bed. Helps her get dressed. Compliments her on her dress and says it's not really necessary to wear that now, it's a bit much for the occasion. And she laughs. Short, fierce bursts of laughter which gust into Maria's tired eyes. And she, Maria, is terrified. Is this Kaline making fun of her? Of her, Maria? Of her eyes? She needs to check them right away.

She places her fingers across her protruding eyeballs. Kaline falls silent the moment Maria positions her forefingers, slightly crooked, from her cheekbones to her frontal bones. Her way of checking whether her eyes have been at work. That's what her father says. If her eyes have been at work again it means that they've come out further. But it's her fingers which should be at work, not her eyes. They should be relaxing in their sockets. While Maria exercises her hands at the piano.

She's always happy when there is no difference between yesterday's inspection and today's. And? Kaline asked. Her eyes felt dry. And a little hard. Sort of like boiled eggs.

And then Kaline told her that a chemise would suffice for her session with the doctor. With a housecoat over that. And she guided Maria's hand to an irresistibly soft material. A velvety soft, very light material. And Maria asserted herself. Insisted on a blouse and bodice for the doctor, held her breath as Kaline tightened the ribbons and laces, let herself be laced up, and pulled her under and outer garments over her head. The cumbersome dress in its entirety.

She insisted on it. Silently. And Kaline helped her. Silently, too. For which she was thankful.

Thanks, thanks. This thanks was spinning around her head, without her uttering it. Until it was too late for thanks. Too late, like a missed cue. But some things, she knows, are communicated without being said. Was her thanks one of these? She's not absolutely sure.

Now Kaline offered her a scent to mask the smell of sleep.

The smell of sleep, that unsavoury smell. From the realm of disgusting things. Best known to her from the sounds her friend makes.

Disgust begins with ugh. Just as relishing nice smells begins with mmmhs and aaahs. When Kaline dabs her face with scent-covered fingers. And sneaks behind her ears, on the shoulders, wrists, between her breasts. In those places where a young lady should be fragrant. Like the flowers in her parents' garden. Which she picks and pushes between her lips. Separating the petals with her tongue. One after another. Feeling them go limp. She doesn't spit them out, but draws them into her mouth. Until they stick to her palate. Where she stores them with her tongue. So that at least she can taste something. The taste of green. Yellow. Pink. Should she now say how exciting it is to know that you are perfumed, and also know the words to express this, but not how you smell? Nor how you look, where you are, or how you are.

She said yes to Kaline straight away. When Kaline offered her this scent with the familiar-sounding name of lavender–rose water. To help combat the discomfort. The strangeness of the house. She said yes because she likes Kaline's hands which are now dabbing the scent on her. There's something else which might help. She asks Kaline to put on her headdress.

Even though Kaline admits that she's no hairdresser, she thinks the headdress is unnecessary and says so, too. Loud and clear. The headdress really isn't necessary now. All she needs is her own head for the session with the doctor. But Maria's own head doesn't yield. With its unequivocal silence. A silence which Kaline hears and understands perfectly well. As most people do. But now, at this moment, with the doctor who's waiting for her to say something, she would prefer not to be silent. She would rather speak. And cannot find a beginning. Not a beginning she can trust. A beginning which would take her somewhere other than around in circles. She's not as speedy as Kaline who said, fine. But let's do it quickly. And brings over the hair. Laughing. While her hands remain serious. Hands that Maria likes.

Kaline's hands know what they're doing. They do not laugh without reason. Sometimes she prefers a person's hands to the individual they're attached to. She thinks of her last doctor. Dr Barth. Eye, cataract and needle specialist. She liked him. She trusted his hands. They were very light. Cold and slightly hard. But she trusted them because they touched Maria as if they'd never touched anything before but Maria. You could trust his hands. But his ideas scared her. And gradually he pulled his ideas over his hands, if that sort of thing is possible. He tried them on like custom-made gloves. What sort of nonsense is going through her head again? Kaline's hands are there to recede behind Kaline's ideas. They perform their work as if this work were what Kaline and she had in common. And not the payment that Kaline gets for it. Very different from her parents' housemaid. Whose hands are hard and pointed. And dry like the dried insects she finds in winter in the nooks and crannies of their house. Which they call the Rüssel. She collects the butterfly wings, spiders' legs, dried hornets, bees and wasps in a little stone box. Her nature collection. Which she calls the *Rüsselchen*. She has a pet name for the hands of her parents' housemaid: winter hands. They obey her parents' commands. As if her, Maria's wishes, were second-class wishes. Foolish, blind peasant's wishes.

Should she say that Kaline's hands are like her friend's? Who she used to play with in the garden. Climbing trees. Until they fell from the trees and fell to the ground. With laughter, with tiredness. Lying there together in the meadow. Holding hands. Brushing hair out of each other's face.

Lying about, the mother scolds, you're lying about in the grass again. Lying about means grass stains. Spiteful, spiteful. She can't see them and can't feel them. Only their dire consequences: at dinnertime she's sent straight to her bedroom.

But, after a copious breakfast Kaline took her by the hand and led her to the treatment room. Listening to her footsteps, Maria immediately tried to identify a familiar sound. A place she had already passed yesterday. When Mesmer showed her and her parents through the house.

And then she recognizes the carpet they're walking over. And Kaline suddenly pulls her hand downwards. And it comes into contact with something wet, warm, soft, silky. Something she cannot get a grip on. Panting loudly. Wriggling wildly.

The doctor's dog is black, Kaline says. Jet-black. And Maria swiftly pulls her hands above her head. And notices that they don't reach to the top of her headdress. But dogs' muzzles and human hands should be kept apart. Should she say how sorry she feels for the doctor? Because if you have to have a dog, then white dogs, as her mother says, are more beautiful than black ones, and altogether nobler, lovelier, more loyal.

And then she lets Kaline take her further on. And now each step is accompanied by the clattering of four paws. And suddenly another noise blends in. A new noise. And she stops at once. Wanting to know if Kaline can hear it, too.

And Kaline is worried that the young lady might be feeling unwell.

No, no. The young lady is feeling absolutely fine. She just has a sense she's dreaming. She can hear these sounds. And that might mean that her ears have become independent. Wouldn't be the first time. And rather menacing. Her body's forever trying to make itself independent. Without considering her. Now and again it produces sounds in her head. A type of music. Like just now, at this very moment. And she says: Sounds that seem to be coming from far away. Spherical sounds. As if not of this earth. Kaline bursts out laughing and pulls her on further.

And the notes are getting ever louder. Until Kaline opens a door. And Maria realizes that she's not dreaming.

She hears Kaline whisper that Doctor Mesmer mustn't be disturbed when he's playing the glass armonica. She certainly didn't want to disturb him. Just wanted to hear these notes which take flight before they've properly settled.

And then a fading polyphony. Which note did she actually hear last? She could ask the doctor now.

But then he will question her hearing which is absolutely perfect . . . She knew it: she's going round in circles. For some time now, for at least . . .

✦ CHAPTER SIX ✦

24 January, 1777
12.30 p.m.

✦✦✦

Does she go around like this every day? He interrupts her silence.

She shrugs, smiles.

He pleads with her to talk to him. To start now. He wants to hear her voice. What she's saying. And the sound. It will help. So does she go around like this every day?

He expected her to remain silent. Just as he expects her to speak as soon as he's standing behind her. Raising his arms until his hands are hovering above her – above her towering hair.

He could really do with the library stool which becomes a three-rung ladder when you open it out. It's in the drawing room, behind the curtain. But – he doesn't want to interrupt things now. Even if it's hard work keeping his hands above her. Cursed Kaline.

He glides his hands through the air to the side of the girl. It feels good to be able to lower his heavy arms. Along this current, the current between his hands and her skin.

So does she go around like this every day?

Yes.

Yes? he says. Yes?

Yes. Or what does he mean? Go around like what?

With an extensive wardrobe and hairpiece.

The tower on her head sways gently from right to left.

So?

No, she says.

He waits a while then raises his hands again. Holds them until they become heavy and glides down through the air without touching the girl.

She's wearing this beautiful headdress for him, she says. On her mother's recommendation. A beautiful headdress is just polite. Like saying please and thank you. Normally she wears a silk cloth around her head at home, when they don't have visitors.

He wonders whether she doesn't find it burdensome always going around with her head covered. A girl of her age . . . a young lady, he corrects himself, could surely show her hair . . .

She must have beautiful thick hair. Dark, he would say . . .

Dark, yes, she says. Brunette with a slight tinge of red. Copper.

That's what they look like. The genteel young ladies from Vienna, he thinks. Dark-blue eyes, copper hair and skin like white silk in front of a cold blue background . . . And fists clenched, he thinks, glancing at her hands.

She wears the cloth around her head to stop getting

cold, she says. She's very sensitive. To everything. Especially draughts.

Her left shoulder starts twitching when she says that in the Rüssel it's as draughty as in an ice house. But as her parents frequently had visitors, she frequently wore the hairpiece. The solid material of the headdress in combination with the large amount of hair attached to it was a bulwark against the draught. Whenever possible, she says. If I'm not ill I wear it.

Too ill? he says. Too ill for a wig?

Too weak, she says. Sometimes she feels terribly weak.

Right, he says, feeling a paralysis in his arms. Trembling as they defy gravity. Falling inexorably. Towards the wig.

As there aren't any guests here, he says quickly, he'll take the headdress off now.

She raises her hands defensively. Not necessary.

His right biceps is burning, contracting, he stretches it to avoid getting cramp.

Yes, he says sternly. Yes it is.

As you wish. She sounds like an automaton.

No, not as he wishes. She should do it for herself, he says impassively. Not for anybody else. Come on, tell me. Show me where the pins are.

With her fingers she points out the places and, relieved, he removes them one by one, placing them on the table. Every time he touches it, white powder stirs from the elaborately knotted headdress. He takes down one piece of hair at a time, undoing individual tresses and placing them next to the pins. Gadzooks! Does she have more tresses than a normal person has individual hairs on their head? Finally he lifts off the base of this splendour, the bonnet, which is firmly attached to the bottom layer of hair.

He stares at her head for a brief while. Unable to say anything. Watches a spasm dart across her shoulders.

What's wrong with her head? Why has she been completely shaven?

He repeats his question and repeats it a second time.

Dr von Störck. She says nothing more.

Where do all those scars come from?

Dr von Störck shaved my head.

Tell me about it.

His hands glide along her body. At the right height they are as light as a feather. Just as they have to be to produce a current in something. The Fluid has stopped flowing in this girl. He will make a note of this.

Dr von Störck, she says, attempted a cure. He tried everything.

What, for example?

Medicines.

Which ones?

Black pasque flower to start with, and valerian root.

She laughs suddenly.

Pasque. Sounds like ass. Sometimes it made her as sedate and plodding as an ass. She grew fond of these herbs, she laughs, while giving the impression she might weep at any moment.

Unlike the medicines that followed. Whose names she's forgotten. There was talk of quicksilver. And sulphur. She remembers this. Because wherever there's sulphur, the devil's not far behind. But Dr Störck said she shouldn't worry. Shame that she wasn't able to see the powder. It was snow white. As pure as an angel from heaven. He dissolved this powder in water and gave it to her to drink. She fell over afterwards. And threw up every two hours. She lay in bed with stomach cramps and didn't get up for a fortnight. Semi-conscious. Couldn't eat a thing and her periods stopped. Instead she got pus-filled boils. All over her back. She was only able to lie on her stomach. Occasionally on her side. A ringing in her ears as if she were sitting day and night inside the organ. She thought this was a punishment for having secretly played the organ on occasions. Against her father's wishes. He said that the organ was no instrument for a lady. It was unsuitable . . . He forbade it because of all the moving up and down with the legs to work the pedals. But she loved the organ. Knew no other instrument with such power. So she played in secret, sometimes . . . Then her father also forbade her from taking the medicine again.

After all, she needs her ears for her profession. So Dr Störck tried leeches. Although they didn't cure her, the ringing in her ears vanished. She got her period again. She was a friend of the medicinal worms. As she was of the herbs.

She shivers.

To begin with the cold, slippery skin of the worms felt strange. And the way the leeches crawled around on her belly before biting her. Soon she was able to distinguish one leech from another. She used to hold them in her moist warm hands like cool worry beads.

They all feel different, she says. One larger, the other fatter. One lively, another lazy. And the greed when they are put on your body. Always hungry. Which didn't mean they'd bite immediately. Some took their time. They don't like to bite when a storm's brewing. As if they were afraid of blood during the thunder and lightning. Dr Störck put them into little glass tubes and placed a piece of onion on her body. Then he dissolved a spoonful of sugar in milk. To brush Maria's body with. The moment he let them out of the glass tubes onto her skin, the leeches started biting. They can't resist the sugary milk. They're like the rest of us.

She would have loved to take Dr Störck's leeches home with her. It was her mother who didn't allow it. No leeches from Dr Störck, who she didn't know. Not even those that didn't bite. She gave them names. Divided them into males and females. Played with them, she said. As if they were dolls . . . If only her friends knew! That she played with leeches! She only had to mention the worms and her friends would make themselves scarce. Without reappearing for weeks. Then she'd write them letters to entice them back, inviting them over for sugary milk.

Where on her body did Dr Störck put the leeches? Mesmer wants to know.

Right behind the ears. And here and here.

She points to her temples and chest, belly.

And then?

Nothing.

He waits. Raises his arms once more. Keeps them above her head for a while. Glides slowly downwards.

Nothing? What does nothing mean?

Nothing means she remembers nothing.

That's just what she thinks, he says.

She thinks, she says, that something really terrible happened after that.

Terrible? he says.

She thinks. *Flow hole*. Dr Störck often talked about this. She didn't really understand what it was. She laughs. He shaved her head and covered it with a poultice. She thought her head was going to burst. Her whole skull pounded and suppurated. The worst of it was that nobody else wanted to be in the same room as her. Her friends gave full vent to their disgust and then stayed away just as her period had. Not even an invitation for some sugary milk helped then.

They all said that when they were with her it stank as bad as the drains outside. She was the only one not to smell anything.

My nose, she says, my nose doesn't work.

Had it always been like that? Was she able to recall a smell? No. Not a single one. Smell was a puzzle to her.

The plaster on her head intensified the spasms in her entire body. And her eyes bulged out. It felt as if her head was slowly being squashed. And then, she says, the flashes started. Dr Störck believed that this was her sight coming back. Insisted this was true. Extolled the virtues of the plaster.

She begged him to remove it. But it stayed there until he decided the flashes had nothing to do with her sight. The flashes didn't come from outside! she says. They came from right inside my head. Ghastly, she says.

After eight weeks of pus and stench and unbearable pain Dr Störck finally removed the plaster. Not cured, but she felt as if she were born again. Just happy to be free of the torture. She couldn't guess what was coming . . .

She breaks off.

Go on, he says.

How warm his hands have become from gliding them through the air. And how soft and light they feel. Like the long fins of some fish.

Dr Störck attached something to her head.

What? he wants to know.

A machine, she says. An electrical one. His newest invention . . .

He interrupts her: Is that what Störck said?

What?

That he'd invented the machine?

She wasn't sure, she said.

Please try to remember precisely, he says. It's important.

It may have been her father. She can't remember. Nothing remained from that period apart from the sensation of a searing pain. A great clump of pain, starting out from her eyes and rolling through her entire body. Which then became liquid and formed a heavy lake.

Where? he says, she should show him the spot.

Here.

She points to her chest, falls silent, slumps.

Go on, he says. Keep talking.

First he said he'd tease sparks out of her. And what a shame that she couldn't see them, these wonderfully shining sparks. But she did hear them, she says. And that was enough. She couldn't imagine a worse sound that that crackling. Clearly the sparks didn't do any good, she says, because he started thumping her.

She tried to persuade herself that the pain was not to no avail. Such intense pain must have a purpose. An effect. It was not just anybody they'd appointed to treat her, but Doctor von Störck. The empress's personal physician! An educated, intelligent man . . . who had produced such an unusual invention . . .

Mesmer interrupts once more. Harshly.

Herr von Störck did not invent the electrostatic machine! If that's what he's claiming then he's a . . .

Yes?

. . . liar . . .

She'll bear that in mind, she says.

Everybody was convinced that she'd soon recover her sight. But the opposite was true. The headaches and the pressure on her eyes became unbearable.

Whenever she stroked her eyes with her hands, they were so hard and bulging that she thought she was in the imperial menagerie, stroking the empress's turtles. And she could barely close them. Her lids were three times as thick as usual. And the insides of her eyes dry, inflamed. And her head a desert.

The desert from the Holy Book. From which her father read to her every evening. The worse she felt, the more she needed the word of God. And the sight of her revolted everybody. Nobody wanted to see me. Nobody wanted to listen to her. They only listened to the doctor. Who interpreted her condition as an initial deterioration.

She doesn't say that she lost her respect for this Herr von Störck. Nor that she was sometimes so scared of him that she refused to get into the carriage, which was meant to take her to him. His ideas gave her such fear.

Fear, but hope.

But there came a point where she just hoped he'd realize how futile his therapy was. Her hopes were in vain. Dr von Störck realized nothing.

He kept on strapping this thing to her head. On her swollen eyes. With every surge of current came a shower of flashes and sparks. And hellish pain. Endless surges, one right after another.

How many? Mesmer is happy that she's talking.

Don't know, she says. Once she counted to one hundred. Not further. Never before had she counted for so long through such pain. She sobs. Unable to breathe for a few seconds. Maybe he should terminate this first session. But he is dying to ask a final question.

Did the empress know of this?

The empress knows everything she wants to know, she says. Does he think the empress ought to know about it?

Oh yes, he says, absolutely she should be told about it.

Why does he say that?

He hesitates. He had not counted on this question.

Does she actually want to see?

She freezes, says she'll answer him even though he's brushed away her question with his own. Of course she'd like to see. Absolutely she would.

After all that friends and relatives have told her, seeing must be the loveliest activity there is. Lovelier than speaking and singing. Although singing is definitely one of the loveliest.

And she wants to play the piano. For a professional career you need eyes. If you can't see, you can't be seen either. If you can't be seen, you can't be heard. If you can't be heard, you're not alive. That's what her father says. And she totally agrees with him. She wants to travel. To Italy and England. Become famous. Throughout Europe. Maybe in America, too. She wants to play large concerts to foreigners. In foreign cities. She wants to know what they look like. What people look like. And animals. She wants to appear with magnificent coiffures, in elegant dresses and look people in the eye.

Does that mean more to her than being seen? he asks.

He might think that she's saying . . . asking for too much. Or. However, she adds, if every therapy is so painful she'd rather stay blind.

She cries. Says she's upset.

They can measure the distance and course of the sun, as well as of the moon and the stars, and the height of mountains. They can divide up the year and the hours. The globe, the sea, the mountain ranges and ships. And can say that this tower, that palace needs foundations so deep and so wide to last centuries. But can't anybody help her? It's difficult to understand.

I can feel myself, she says, drifting further and further away, from people and the earth. Without ever having seen them . . . Further than the moon, further than the stars. Maybe I'm no longer reachable. Every pain drives me a little further from the earth. And from people . . .

He understands, Mesmer says. She should be happy to have survived her medical treatments. These days the most important thing for a patient is to survive the doctor's visit.

Anybody who survives medicines and treatments has a good chance of getting better again.

She can't understand, she says, how he can talk like that. He's a doctor himself, after all.

Yes, he's a doctor. And he undertakes research as a doctor. And thus he knows that there are doctors and doctors. And doctors and doctors are not the same thing.

She doesn't understand this at all.

Doesn't matter, he says. She has nothing to fear with him. He won't prescribe her any dangerous medicines. To start with an infusion of *Chamomilla* and *Pulsatilla nigricans*, twice a day, and in the evenings an infusion of *Radix valerianae* ... Leeches ... definitely. And a session at the magnetic baquet every other day. In addition to her individual magnetic treatments. The key thing is that she tells him everything. He's on her side.

She seems to consider what he is saying.

She should tell him everything she's feeling or thinking, he says. And without embarrassment. Anything. He wants to know even the most meaningless thoughts. They do have a meaning, maybe only for her and her life. But he was part of that now, too. So they had a meaning for him, too. She must therefore confide everything to him ... Even if that made him sound like her confessor.

She'd been freezing the whole morning, the girl says out of the blue. And now she was suddenly feeling warm.

It's perfectly normal, he says, letting his hands drop to her shoulders.

There is a brief and fierce knocking at the door, which then flies open. Anna, a jug in her hands and a quiver in her voice.

She didn't wish to disturb. Just brought some water.

Instinctively he's taken his hands away. As if he'd been caught doing something untoward. Anna is standing in the room. Fire in her eyes. Then she cools down. Her horror at the sight of the bald, scarred young lady. He shakes his head. Gesticulates. She should go. Now. She answers with a disappointed: Why?

He puts his finger to his lips. She must be quiet. She crashes the jug down on the table so the water sloshes over the edge.

What a lovely, compelling case, she says loudly. An absolute star. She just wanted to take a look. She wanted to learn something, she said. She was his pupil after all. Did the young lady mind if she, Anna Maria, Mesmer's wife and pupil, watched the master at work?

The girl, slumped, doesn't reply.

That's enough. Before he'd even uttered it his wife had slammed the door shut from outside the room. The girl has put her hands over her face.

She's feeling pain, she says. As intense as the flashes.

She ignores his question of where, as well as his advice that she needs some rest now.

She doesn't want any more pain. She sobs. He promised her . . . She hasn't played the piano yet . . . Where is her headdress?

She gets up. Doesn't know where to go. Turns around, banging her hip into the table, leans over the table, feeling for her wig. Finds it. Tries to reassemble the hair pieces on her head. Fiddles with the tresses, stirring up dust which makes her cough and sneeze and snivel all at once. Until he touches her shoulder. Takes the hair from her hand and promises to bring her to her room right away.

Not to my room, she shouts. To the piano.

He takes her. As he leaves he can hear her racing through the scales. Once more with this power which is well suited to the English instrument. And she is even modulating it.

⤙ CHAPTER SEVEN ⤚

28 January, 1777

When she wakes a hand is in hers. An unfamiliar one. A dainty, cool, dry hand. Feminine man or masculine woman. Can't decide. Light fingers which she squeezes and which withdraw immediately. Lovely. Every nice hand is a potential friend. For her collection. Stupid that she doesn't have her friendship book with her. She tries to sit up. Her head is heavy. Are there stones tied to it? Not just her head. Her arms and legs. Her feet. Nothing but weight.

Don't be frightened. She knows the voice that goes with the hand. Of course. She could have guessed. Musician's hands. Violinist's hands. Riedinger, who says the doctor's put magnets on her. And how does she feel?

She's just trying to work that out. By recalling what happened and how she ended up here. On this mattress.

It had been the eighth day. She remembers that. She'd woken early and, still half-asleep, rubbed her face, and gone through her ritual of rubbing the sleep from her eyes. The shock that she hadn't found the usual. No turtles, no hard-boiled eggs. No swelling. Or was she mistaken? Soft eyes, softer than the wax from the candles which she immediately lit so that Kaline could see what she could no longer feel. She had turned the chair towards the door, sat down. Listened out for Kaline's unmistakably light steps which always sound as if she's dragging two long wings behind her.

Kaline had burst into the room with a piece of news that unsettled her further: Today the young lady would be able to join in at the magnetic baquet, she announced, carrying the washing basin past Maria to the dressing table. With the other patients, she says. Count Pellegrini, sweet little Kornmann, the Duchess of Kingston, and of course Mistress Ossine. And whoever else might come from outside today, they'd see . . .

Maria had turned her head towards her. Put her hands back up to her eyes. She could hardly feel them with her fingers. Were her fingers deceiving her? Had they become blind for her blind eyes? Or was Kaline blind? Failing to notice her eyes and wringing out the sponge instead. It definitely wasn't the doctor. He'd see at once that her eyes had retreated into their sockets overnight. She'd asked Kaline to take her straight to the treatment room. She could have easily found the way there herself. But Kaline needn't know that.

She recalls that Kaline had not been in favour. The musicians wouldn't be there for another hour. And the doctor not for an hour and a half. And wouldn't a few splashes of water on her skin freshen her up? And she recalls that she had played her most effective card. She had run to the door and said nothing. Upon which Kaline had taken her by the hand.

80

She had wandered round the magnetic baquet in the treatment room. Several times. Been amazed by how small it was,
and that the second and third time it seemed a little larger. She
had paced in all directions and tried out all the possible seats.
To the door and back. Onto the musicians' podium and down
again. Had felt the velvet covered walls, the mirrors and the
magnetic equipment. The iron rods in their holders. Had gone
every which way, to try everything out and find the right
seat. Where the doctor would not be able to miss her. What
would he say? She had decided on a seat, her seat, the seat
with the best acoustics. All she knew about the other patients
were a few names. But what did that matter? None of them
would be able to ask her about her eyes.

Excuse me, do my eyes look different today?

Different? Different from when?

From yesterday evening.

She recalls the woman's voice wishing her good morning
as if from nowhere, but making it sound as if it were the most
wretched morning imaginable. A voice which could not mean
what it was saying. She recognized it. The woman who had
screamed the place down a few days ago.

Her name was Ossine. Her neighbour.

Happy to be alone with her, because if no one else was
there she could ask. She asked whether she might ask her a
question.

Please go ahead.

What actually happened a few days ago? She'd been there
when Ossine had her crisis. She'd screamed as if . . . as if
she'd been impaled. Alive. She was new here today and was

frightened of sitting at the magnetic baquet. It was bound to be painful.

Oh, and she recalls very well the look that Mistress Ossine had given her. She can feel those looks on her skin. Like stings. Or volleys of stones. It had clearly been the wrong question.

What made the young girl come out with such nonsense? Pain, sure, everybody here had pains in various places. That's why we're here. And crisis – so what? Everyone has a crisis sooner or later. That's another reason why they're here. But it was a malicious insinuation that she'd been screaming loudly. She was no madwoman. She was a lady. Which meant she had self-control. Even if she often felt like screaming. Last night, for example. She hadn't slept a wink. A creaking kept her awake. Heavy footsteps. Beelzebub himself. The only thing was, she said, the footsteps came from next door. From Maria's room. Why on earth was Maria stomping round her room so noisily in the middle of the night? She really ought to ask the doctor for a sleeping draught. The doctor could think of something for everybody, no doubt for her, too. And had she ever tried theriac?

A long time ago, Maria said. She was surprised. She hadn't even been on the chamber pot in the night. Maybe she'd slept too deeply. Maybe her snoring had penetrated the walls. Like her father sometimes. You never hear it yourself. Only other people. Maybe that's what Ossine heard. Her nose gets so blocked up at night that she has to breathe through her mouth to avoid suffocating.

Ossine's suspicions point in another direction. She was scared that Beelzebub was going into Maria's room without her noticing. That's really very bad. Maybe she ought to call in another specialist besides Dr Mesmer . . .

But Maria was able to reassure her on this point. Her conscience was the most steadfast thing about her. Free of major sins, at any rate. And the minor sins, all her wishes, jealousies and yearnings were regularly purified at the confessional in the Stephanskirche.

She didn't imagine that Maria's sin count was low, Mistress Ossine carped, at the very moment that the musicians came in, followed by the other resident patients. Ossine seemed inspired. It might be dark in the room, she said so loudly that everybody could hear, but not so dark that you couldn't see there was something not quite right with Maria's eyes.

At that moment, she recalls, she couldn't feel her eyes any more and she got a dreadful fright.

Ossine said that practically all she could see were the whites of her eyes. The pupils were shooting in all directions like crazy bumblebees.

And an unfamiliar man's voice piped up. Oh God, you're right. Should they call the doctor?

Maria's hands had located her inexplicable eyes, again slightly swollen. The inexplicable tears, her face wet but she wasn't crying.

There was something up with this girl. Ossine turned to everyone in the room, she'd sensed that immediately, she said. It was not for nothing that she walked around in circles uncontrollably in her sleep.

She recalls that an unfamiliar hand had touched her arm, a hairy, coarse hand, and that she'd instinctively struck out at

83

it. Struck three times in quick succession, while the unfamiliar hand tried to catch hold of hers.

Excuse me, a man's voice said. He'd forgotten to introduce himself. Count Pellegrini. He'd heard a lot about her . . .

Meanwhile Ossine called out: That savage girl must compose herself. Get the doctor, quick!

And she recalls that the attention of one of the musicians had been captured. His name was Riedinger. What was going on here?

The same friendly voice that's now sitting beside her, saying she doesn't have to remember everything. It's normal to forget one's sleep.

And she: she wants to remember, however.

Ossine said that, even though there weren't set places at the baquet, the girl was sitting exactly where she, Ossine, had been for the past fortnight. Between Count Pellegrini and little Benjamin Kornmann.

Ce n'est pas un problème, she heard the treble of a boy's voice say.

And Riedinger. Surely there was no malicious intent. Just an oversight, he'd said.

An oversight due to blindness! Ossine had raised her voice. She'd find herself a new seat. She just wanted to say it, she said, so as not to deprive Maria of the opportunity to learn her lesson.

And little Kornmann chipped in that his father would be coming to collect him. In the next few days. Maybe even today. Then Mistress Ossine could have his place.

No thanks, Ossine said. For safety's sake there must be a gap between her and the girl who can't see anything. Because otherwise she, Ossine, will think about it constantly. It's not worth the fuss.

Well, everything's fine then, isn't it? Riedinger said.

She recalls that after this painful episode she'd stood up. And Riedinger said she should stay where she was.

Yes, stay there, Ossine said. Too late was too late. She'd give up the seat. Maria could keep it.

She recalls feeling unsure. She'd wanted to sit, but stayed standing while Ossine settled down opposite her. She stood there for ages. And also ignored little Kornmann, who whispered: When his father comes, this horrid Ossine won't know what's hit her. His papa will tear strips off her.

She stood until the musicians began tuning their instruments. And all the patients took their seats. She recalls registering every Good Morning, dividing the voices into good and wicked, into friendly and unfriendly, and appreciating that this division was unfounded. She recalls that she lost the thread. And phrases raced through her head. And that she was worried that she might say them out loud.

That's my seat. I feel it. Places resonate. And I hear them. I'm a musician. And I heard Ossine scream. For heaven's sake. There are witnesses, too. Ossine was screaming blue murder. Even though she won't believe it herself.

When all was quiet around her and she realized that she wouldn't say any of her phrases out loud, she fell into the chair. Ossine's reproaches were hanging in the room. Right amongst the strangers. Another missed entry. How many was that now, she thought, since her arrival? Oh, if only life were a fugue. No voice would lose out.

She was surprised that everyone was silent. As if sitting in a circle were a type of magic that kept mouths closed. She recalls one final interruption. A final latecomer. Small, rapid footsteps, clacking shoes doing a woman's gallop. Fear of arriving too late. Of missing something. Where was Doctor Mesmer, please? She had felt the wind turn around, and with it people's heads.

Riedinger pointed the latecomer to the last free seat. The doctor would be here soon. She recalls the hesitancy in the woman's voice.

She needed to speak with the doctor. It was important.

Sorry? What about? Please take a seat.

She didn't want to sit.

Riedinger guessed it was a back complaint and said they'd surely find a solution.

Yes, she said. No . . . he was mistaken. Sitting wasn't the problem. It was just . . . here. Sitting here was the problem.

She recalls the tension in the room.

Not . . . with these . . . people. You don't know who I am, do you? she added.

The patients were whispering to each other. But when Mesmer's footsteps and voice were audible it fell silent at a stroke.

There's only one baquet in this house, he said. People who refuse to take a seat at it won't get any magnetic therapy.

He surely had no idea who he had before him.

He knew very well and he was delighted to welcome Marquise von Müller. He requested her to take a seat so that they could get started.

86

She insisted on a separate baquet!

She could insist all she liked, he said. It won't change a thing. There was no separate baquet.

Then he should install one, she said. One for people of her kind. Appropriate to their station.

In summer he'll set up a number of baquets. Outside, he said, in the park, beneath the trees. Then she'd be able to choose which baquet she wanted to sit at. But from experience he could tell her that trees had very little interest in people's backgrounds. Trees let all sorts of people sit beneath them.

Winter or summer, inside or out, she would never sit with such vermin. So?

She waited. They all waited.

No, Mesmer said. Even if he set up five baquets. His answer was no.

Was that his final word?

His very final one.

She recalls the swishing, as if the lady had torn a hole in the air which closed again only slowly. Some patients laughed, others clapped their hands. When she slammed the door: silence.

She recalls feeling uncertain as to what to make of this scene. And pleased that her parents knew nothing of it.

Like all the others, she had waited for the doctor to break the tension. But he didn't break it; he pushed it to one side as you might push aside a curtain. And behind it another curtain appears. And so on. Mesmer did his round. Patient by patient. Whispered to all of them. The whispering gave rise to further tension. And she thought of those occasions when she used to sit outside in the garden or, when she went on excursions with her parents, in the fields, and thought she could hear the flowers growing. The flowers, the corn. A cornfield shooting upwards.

Standing behind her, he had placed his hands on her shoulders. They were light and warm. The feeling as if she'd been in chains which were now slipping off her. She let herself go, everything she was at that very moment. She recalls having wished for this for a long time. Since the first handshake. No, even before that. She felt secure. The room snuggled up to her. Now, here. Her place. There was nowhere else. Now all he had to do was ask her about her eyes . . .

How had she slept? he wanted to know. And how did she feel?

She whispered, Excellently.

He couldn't see her eyes. He was behind her, after all. And it occurred to her that it was dark in here. And dark means that people cannot see anything. And if people cannot see anything they're blind. And stupid.

She let him put an iron rod into her hand. She should use it to touch those areas where she was in most discomfort. Where she had pain.

Pain? She didn't feel any, she murmured. That was yesterday. Today the swelling in her eyes had gone down!

But he kept on talking: In the next few days she should come for an individual session. He left her with the iron rod.

In the next few days. So not today. And probably not tomorrow. Maybe the day after. Or the day after that. But she will meet with him in the light. She will stand before him until he can't help but see her. She tried out the rod. Pointed it to

88

her chest, belly, head. To her heart. And her navel. To the crook of her arm. She sat up straight. Lowered her head. Head and iron rod. Eyes and iron rod. Throat and iron rod. Nothing but funny pairings, she thought, bringing it to her right eye then her left. Finally she used it to support her head. Right between her two eyes, where her eyebrows met. Could she feel anything? A jet spouting forth from the iron rod. Onto her eyes. Pleasantly cool. And around her a hushed silence – as in church – which ended with Mesmer's announcement.

They were all to join hands. And move closer together. And then: Haydn!

The count took her left hand with his hairy paw. She recalls wondering briefly which body parts he had put his rod to, where his pain was, and bet it was his belly. There were times when it would be good to have eyes! But even without them she could feel the fragile equilibrium in the circle.

Can you feel it? Can you feel it? The count tickled her hand. It's coming . . .

What?

The wave . . .

A stern Shhh! from the Kornmann boy.

Then the wave took hold of the group. A gentle tilting, rising, falling, climbing. Maria thought she could feel each twitch in the circle. As if every heartbeat were assembling inside her and reproducing. They all rocked and swayed. A small, delicate movement, which came as much from outside as from within. And in her eyes something she had never felt before: as if a soft paintbrush were swishing around inside. Or was it fish fins?

The ones her geography tutor had told her about. When she, feeling along wires, followed the course of the Danube on the map. Every curve in the wire a bend in the river, every bend in the river a feeling of happiness. This Danube with its trout and char cheerfully fanning themselves on the river bed. They let the water flow past their cold bodies. And then they go into fishermen's nets. Her tutor had told her a little about this – an incredibly fine mesh. She was horrified. And then the victim: a fresh, clammy, slippery trout. Feeling as if it wanted nobody to touch it: my hands aren't water, after all. She recalls having said this. And later, on Friday, the trout ended up on the lunch table of her religious parents, and they'd eaten it together.

She recalls all of them swaying rhythmically in a single, gentle, harmonic underwater movement to the music, and she, Maria, doing it with them. And a feeling as if there were neither a beginning nor an end, only being carried along by the music. By her music. By Haydn. And by this violinist. Riedinger. She'd remembered his name. His playing. Riedinger's violin sounded human. As if the body of the instrument were not wooden, but skin and flesh and bones. And female. A singing girl. A singing woman, she thinks. A singing fish. At once sad and buoyant. She recalls wanting to sing along. Wanting to laugh. About herself. And thinking that if she laughed out loud about herself it would mean she was happy. She didn't dare do it. But this didn't bother her. It's what's familiar that makes you happy.

She recalls a fish, the biblical whale, Count Pellegrini, starting to snort beside her. And that she'd scarcely been able to suppress her laughter. Thinking she was not so steadfast after all, as she laughed about his chest, this instrument with a hundred chambers. In which it growled, rumbled, rattled. Resonance chambers which she could not pinpoint in her own body. While, next to her, little Kornmann started to hum like a girl, humming higher and higher until it sounded insect-like. Until from right opposite her a loud moaning drowned everything out. Rising to become a scream, before the jolly Haydn melody had faded away. Ossine. Faster than any presto. Squeezing the scream out of her body. While also holding tightly onto it. Fighting. Every scream a victory. Muffling the others. They all fought with themselves. With their bodies and corsets.

Ossine was the winner. The first, the loudest, the deepest of all.

O God. Maria could hear the cats that would wail on the roofs and walls when on heat. She could hear the word, the only word in her family for this: indecent. A torture to play with this going on. No musician deserves this. Then. To her horror she had felt her eyes careering out of control. Itching and burning. Waves of spasms rolled across her face. She was utterly defenceless. Her head was yanked upwards. She let everything go. The iron rod crashed to the floor. A hairy hand grasped for hers, but grasped thin air. She rubbed her eyes. Wanted to scream. Could not. But then she could. Spasms jerked her in all directions. And she recalls that, all of a sudden, the music went silent. And three men came running towards Ossine. The doctor at the front. Ossine's screams penetrated Maria; she felt as if her body were a gigantic ear ready to burst at any moment if she didn't submit. And then, how good it felt to submit. And everybody ran over to her.

She recalls the doctor running past Ossine and over to her. She recalls the musicians' hands taking hold of her. She recalls thinking that now she was their instrument they were rapidly but gently manoeuvring out of the room. Away from the ears of the group. Accompanied by a faintly vibrating jealousy of the attention she was receiving. And of the doctor. While Ossine's bloodcurdling screams faded away. Then nothing more.

She'd probably been taken to the adjoining room. (She'd worked out the way there a long time ago. Had felt her way there. Had been there.) Maybe Riedinger had held her.

She's forgotten, just as one forgets a dream on awakening.

Arms and legs are heavy, they want to stretch. Everything's heavy.

Riedinger says the doctor tied magnets to her body while she was asleep.

What's going on here? She's surprised she feels so tired after having slept.

That's normal. And she needn't talk. Riedinger sounds friendly.

Oh, Riedinger. But she wants to talk. She knows from Kaline that he was a late starter with the violin. Now he's keeping the wolf from the door with Mesmer's magnetic baquet.

She's still completely bewitched by his violin, she says. It's a good thing he's here.

He'd rather have a position in the court orchestra, he says. Or go on a concert tour. He spreads a blanket over her.

A concert tour? She'd like to do that, too, she says.

There we go. It's out now. Let him think she's mad. Her, a girl! Blind! Wanting to go across Europe!

He's heard a lot about her, he says, but never heard her play.

Would he care to accompany her on the violin?

He'd be delighted.

She suggests Koželuh, her tutor. A symphony. Beautiful violin part. Not particularly easy.

Has she got the score?

She doesn't need any scores. She plays by ear.

How does she learn new pieces then?

She has two pianofortes at home. Side by side in the drawing room. Koželuh plays on one. She on the other. He starts by playing the entire piece. She listens. Then he plays it bar by bar. And she copies him.

But she'll get a score for him, Riedinger. She'll send a message to her parents.

He's looking forward to it, he says. In a tone she believes implicitly.

93

⊰ CHAPTER EIGHT ⊱

31 January, 1777

Should he warn her? Some patients experience pain when stroked magnetically. Others have convulsions, experience numbness or fall unconscious. Some develop secret feelings. But nothing permanent.

Maria is stronger than she thinks. Better just start. Without saying much. Words distract. And Maria reacts strongly to words. As if they were pain.

When he comes in she's sitting already.

He sits down in front of her. Face to face. The right side of her body opposite his left. He's putting himself in harmony with her. Locking the poles briefly.

He'll place his hands on her shoulders. Stroke her arms down to her fingertips. Hold her thumbs momentarily. Repeat everything. Twice, three times. In this way he'll set up currents from her head to her feet. And find out whether the cause of her illness is what he suspects: a blocked spleen.

Whenever he looks at Maria he sees the empress before

him, watching Maria play the piano. Music surging through her. But now, now the empress is bewildered as she looks on. And then he comes into the picture. And points at Maria's eyes.

The eyes, he notes, have receded. A clear success of my magnetic treatment. He notes that the dog is sitting beside Maria. The fact that she's letting it put its head in her lap is another change in the right direction. Her nerves are gradually relaxing. No part of her chemise disguises the fullness of her figure. She's fat. Not that he is averse to plump women. She is the epitome of a patient. The blocked fluid is causing the bulging, bloating, swelling and denting on her body. And: dark stubble is growing on her head. Extraordinary, he notes, the complete physical (not mental!) listlessness as soon as there's no instrument in sight . . . No, he corrects himself, in earshot/reach. New today, he notes, the neck strangely thrust forward. Then he underlines: The receded eyes are proof that my method works.

Nobody can take that away from him. The living proof is sitting before him. Hopefully the empress will remember what Maria's eyes used to look like. Eyes forget more quickly than ears. He ought to have had a drawing made of Maria. Why didn't he persuade Messerschmidt to do a few sketches of her, or make a plaster model of her haggard face? Today, on the tenth day, it's already too late. An unambiguously ambiguous result, a huge missed opportunity and a huge success!

He sees the empress gradually realize how much she needs Mesmer. What if she commands him to establish a school? Pass on his method. Instruct apprentice doctors. Train them according to his model: himself. Because she considers him to be a paragon of humanity. He, the model human being. He will be venerated. His pupils will be called *the ministers* of the community. The priest will introduce them. Down to the tiniest parish. And Mesmer will supervise everything relating to the happiness and advancement of the human race. He is not merely a doctor. He is a teacher, advisor, decision-maker and reconciler of his fellow citizens. And, of course, guardian of their health. Nobody gets past Mesmer. Least of all Mesmer himself.

He has scarcely begun when Maria starts spouting forth. Her soprano voice crystal clear and bright.

She says she's extremely alert. Since yesterday morning. Since the session in the magnetic baquet. Nothing escapes her, not the slightest thing. And everything turns to music in her head. Can you hear the dripping? she says. All that rapid dripping?

The snow's melting, he says. How slowly he speaks compared to her. Full moon yesterday, so a change in the weather today, an onset of warmth, a thaw . . .

The house, she interrupts, one large dripping orchestra. It's dripping from every corner, from every sill and ledge, and it's dripping onto every surface and running down the walls. And they're sitting here in the dry, and it makes her feel so cheerful, she says. She can feel it with her whole body, in a strange way she doesn't recognize. It's almost distressing, she says. All these rhythms from all points of the compass. Slowly from back there, and much more quickly from over there. And a whole staccato to itself way over there. Sometimes *crescendo*, sometimes *diminuendo*.

The back of the house is in the shade, Mesmer says. Whereas at the front the snow is melting from the roof.

A snow opera, she says. But what use is that? She can't help write it. At best she can play along. But how can she remember what has been played? Everything's fading away. Without her knowing what it actually was, and what it involved. This is torture for her. Exhausting. This wasted delight.

She's filling up and filling up. Again and again. Like a wet nurse's breasts. Or Prometheus' liver. Her father told her about him. Who gave mankind fire.

She suddenly feels so warm, she says. The warmth is flowing down her body. As when I'm being washed, she says. I'd love to know what water looks like . . . It sounds so lovely. And that's probably how music came about, she says, and dancing. From snow and sun and water. Does he think this, too? And she continues talking. While he strokes down her arms.

Her father thinks differently. Her father says scholars say that music came about together with dancing.

And this all began with a sensitive old man. When he saw a young girl he was filled with divine feelings. He was the first to think about this divine feeling. The girl had been skipping alongside her mother across a meadow, flowers in her hand. Some boys, just as beautiful as she, were chasing her. Playfully, they tried to catch the girl. The old man enjoyed this so much that he wanted to see it over and over again. He asked the children to repeat their game.

All the old men who watched this were delighted. They marvelled at the youngsters and praised them. And the pleasure they had from skipping and the pleasure from the applause produced a natural desire among the children to think out more and more games. And to sing ever better. And so this is how, progressively, music and dance came about. And the story goes on. When the Greeks realized how dancing strengthened the body, making it supple and graceful, their young people were made to dance and sing on all occasions. And then they developed war dances and martial music too.

She pauses briefly. As an entranced Mesmer listens to her he notices that his hands have stopped in the crooks of her arms. He continues to stroke, slowly.

The Sybarites were a people who were expert at horse breeding. They loved dancing so much that they even taught their horses how to dance. This was their undoing, however. For the Crotonians, with whom they were in conflict, had secretly listened to the music of their horse ballets. And when the Sybarite cavalry attacked them, they piped out these same ballets. The Sybarites lost all control over their warhorses, because they started dancing. And thus the horses lost the battle for their masters . . .

Nice story, he says, starting from the front.

Yes, she says, but.

What?

I don't know. If it's true.

That doesn't matter. It's all about music and its effects, he says. And what's truer than the power of these effects?

By true she means whether it happened like that and not differently.

That's not the point of stories. Stories are invented and untruthful. At least most of them are. Anybody could come up with anything. But some, he says, convey a sort of primeval idea. And become true simply through the aptitude of those who understand them. It's not about concepts or whether something actually was like that. Stories like these come from an unconscious drive. Which ultimately only needs to be aroused.

That's over her head, she says.

He doesn't believe it. He read in the newspaper that nothing goes over her head. He shares this opinion.

But, she says, it really is about truth. And things as they are in reality are true. As far as this is concerned, her blindness is a major disadvantage. Because eyes are made for truth, aren't they? To see how something is. At least that's what most of her friends say. One more reason why she wants to see.

He has to disappoint her there, he says. The eyes are no closer to the truth than the other senses. All is lies, illusion and imagination. All senses, including the eyes, invent stories to the best of their ability. As a doctor he experiences this on a daily basis. The important thing is to listen to the stories.

Like music? she says.

Yes, he says, maybe like music.

How had she got onto this in the first place? she says. She's forgotten. That's what she's like. And, incidentally, she doesn't merely feel warm now, but hot. And her nose is starting to run. Does he have a handkerchief? Not one. She needs five.

Five, he makes a mental note, she's asking for five handkerchiefs.

She feels marvellous, she says. Since this morning.

99

Especially her eyes, she says, pointing at them. And now, apart from her nose, she's feeling even better. There must come a point at which she'll feel so good that there can be no better. She's afraid of this point.

Her face turns red, her neck, her *décolleté*.

The heat is fierce. She wants to take a break.

Unperturbed, Mesmer strokes down her arms. Not stopping when she says she feels pain. Her eyes. And where's her headdress? (He needs to make a note of this: When she feels weak the first thing she asks for is her headdress.) She grabs her head.

This stubble field isn't her hair. I've got long hair. Not bristles like this. Like pig bristles they make brushes out of. Her hand is numbed merely by running it over her head.

And he says that in Priestley's opinion hair is in fact tiny horns.

She jerks her hand away. Hits the dog. Flinches when it yelps. Grumbling, it moves to one side. Ruffles its fur with her hands, slides off the chair, landing by the dog. Buries her face in its fur. Panting, the dog gets out of her way, lies down. Seeks out her hands with its muzzle. Licks her hands, her eyes.

The dog, she snivels, is the only one who knows how she's doing.

Then she turns round.

Why's he not saying anything? she shouts.

Her eyes, he says. They've retreated back into their sockets.

Why hadn't he said that earlier? He *is* her doctor, she

says. And she, she's blind after all! She can't see where her eyes are, can she?

She wants to go to the piano right away. He takes her there. Then stands by the door. Listening to an unfamiliar, rather severe piece of music. Could be Haydn. When he looks up, Anna is standing next to him.

She looks at him.

Not now, he says.

When? she says.

Later.

When later?

This evening.

No. She's shouting. Now.

Alright, he says. But not here.

Where then?

Upstairs.

She is so close on his heels it's as if she's driving him up the stairs. Once upstairs the volume gets of control.

She married him.

He's aware of that.

You are my husband.

He's not really looking at her. He's looking through her, as if behind this irate woman there's another waiting for him. His reasonable Anna.

Her husband, her late Lieutenant Colonel Konrad von Posch of the Imperial–Royal supply bureau, taught her how to read and write. Not for nothing, surely. She needed to do something with it. It was her duty. He must be able to teach her something, too. Was that asking too much? She supported him whenever she could. Had the laboratory installed for him. With the latest technology! Who amongst his colleagues had a microscope from de Leeuwenhoeck? In return he could give something back to her, his dear wife. A little of his method.

She should be patient, he says.

How much longer? she says. And what was he thinking, banishing her from the room? From the young lady. Word will soon get around Vienna as to the tone in which Doctor Mesmer permits himself to speak to his wife. Widow of Lieutenant Colonel von Posch of the Imperial–Royal supply bureau. Was he naive?

He raises his hand, drops it. Every gesture makes her even more livid.

Not a problem. Of course he will instruct her.

So why did he throw her out just then? From the young Paradis girl.

He shrugs his shoulders. The wrong moment, he says. As soon as the therapy starts working she can be present. As often as she likes and whenever takes her fancy.

She gives him a searching look. Was that his intention?

What?

To refuse to let her take part in his life? And now lying, too.

He wasn't lying.

Oh yes you are, she says. The therapy has already started working.

What did she mean by that?

Did he think she was blind?

He waits.

The girl's eyes. No longer bulging! If that isn't a success!

After little more than a week! She'd actually wanted to congratulate him. But his behaviour made it difficult . . .

She walks up to him, gives him a hug. He frees himself.

With her dead husband, she says, she produced a son. But he was at the military academy now. So on his own two feet. And she was a good ten years older than him, her Mesmer. Too old for any more children. But . . . she thought . . . the patients . . . could be . . . your and my . . . children.

He had known nothing of her fantasy.

Congratulations, he says. She's a good observer. Something every physician needed to be, too.

So would he show her the trick?

What trick? he says.

The crucial one, she says. The one he uses to control people.

He didn't know what she was talking about.

Yes you do, she says. You know very well. I can tell you know. Just say: Yes.

She threatens to start shouting again.

He pre-empts her. With his yes. Which coincides with a clearing of the throat. Kaline is at the door.

And Anna bellows. What does she think she's doing? Listening in on them.

Please excuse me, Kaline interrupts. The new patient is in a bad state. Awfully bad. She's rolling on the ground in pain, boring her knuckles into her eye-sockets. She, Kaline, is worried that the girl's eyes won't be able to stand the pressure for much longer.

*

The girl is lying beside the piano. On his knees, the Kornmann boy is bending over her. Wafting air over her with her fan. And tracing with his forefinger her fists pressed onto her eyes, the reddened face.

Mesmer sends him out, lights a candle. Speaks her name. No reaction. He sits by her feet. Strokes her knee.

Why's she crying? At the very moment when her eyes are making progress? Isn't she happy?

Show me your eyes. I want to see them.

She takes her hands away, sits up.

Please open your eyes.

She obeys.

He holds the candle to her face. She screams. Her hands dart back to her face, covering it. She topples to the ground on her back. A glimmer of light. It was what he was expecting.

⊰ CHAPTER NINE ⊱

15 February, 1777

~❧~❧~

Light equals pain. Seeing hurts. It has to be like that. If only she'd known it. She would have stayed with her parents. Maybe. Maybe not. Side-effects of seeing. Nobody mentioned this. Not her parents, not the doctor, not her friends. They raved about it. She can still hear their oohs and aahs. Sounds which were almost sung. Hitting the highest registers of squealing. Squealed squeals. From which Maria concluded that seeing must be pure pleasure. But not seeing in itself. People rave about what they see, just as she raves about what people tell her they see. Clothes, flowers, houses, horses, carriages, diamonds and women. They forget the stinging white and the white stings, forget the painful, blinding glistening. Stupid to believe that seeing is as exciting as singing. The singing of the Danube. Maria can sing every day, without hurting herself. After playing the piano, singing is the best. Opening one's breathing. To be caressed on the inside by one's breathing and, on the outside, enveloped by one's voice, together with the space it occupies and everything around. Growing ever larger.

Maria's realm. The blindfold Mesmer has prescribed her doesn't change this one bit. He's is very concerned about her. Five layers of silk, it must be pitch black beneath that. He was wrong. Not even five layers of silk are enough. Through the chinks where the blindfold was wrapped around her nose the light shot up to her eyes.

Mesmer had to seal off the tiny chinks. But how?

He consulted Anna. For two whole days she has been crocheting tiny pads to close the gaps. Experimenting with thread, colour, form. Had the girl sit beside her so she could measure her face.

Said that the black, sausage-shaped ones that were tightly crocheted were the best.

Could they be black and bean-shaped, too? Maria wanted to know.

Why not? Anna wrapped five layers of silk around these black, bean-shaped pads. It felt like flowers. Petals.

As if Mesmer had given her petals.

Maria counts them with her fingers. She had imagined light to be so soft and gentle. Before she encountered it. If that was indeed light she had encountered, with such force that she fell unconscious. It was a declaration of war. No, the light was treacherous. Underhand, like the Prussian king.

A light without a declaration of war. Like Fritz invading Silesia. Her arch-enemy, the light.

She had to be protected from the light. Especially now. In the dazzling early spring. That's what she heard Mesmer say.

His deep voice underpins everything he says. When she

came round again, he talked of the days getting longer and promised her that, if she was appropriately dressed, she'd be able to go for walks when the weather got milder. In the garden. A walk in the garden would bring her into harmony. The snowdrops and spring snowflakes, maybe some crocuses already by the wall of the house.

9 March, 1777

In the morning she'd followed Mesmer up endless stairs. Behind her, Kaline and the coachman, dragging up her coffers and trunks. The stairs groaned, the wood. Her coffers and trunks groaned, Kaline and the coachman.

She's now in the room beneath the roof. The mansard windows are small and nailed up. The coachman said the pigeons would love to live up here. If you let them, they'd move here from the dovecote, making their nests between the timbers and on the sills.

Cooing when she wakes up. Cooing when she goes to sleep. The scratching of small claws on wood. The twisting of feathers when the birds turn round. They sound so close that under her eiderdown she gets the feeling she's lying in a nest with them. Rather close contact with pigeons than with Mistress Ossine. Maria is avoiding her, her catlike footsteps, her voice with a life of its own. So she makes detours. Forgoes breakfast.

As she did this morning. She was in the dining room when she heard some slurping. It was obviously the thick hot chocolate being slurped. Then the cup landed on the saucer. With force, almost smashing its way down. She heard Ossine ask whether she might have another little cup. And a *kipferl*. The voice that doesn't say what it means. It didn't want a little cup. It wanted a jug. A whole jug of hot chocolate and a basket of *kipferl*. Some people are made of nothing but holes. Never sated by anything. Everything falls straight through them, vanishing from the world. Ossine was one of these. A sort of end of the world. Even if there appears to be no end of the world on a globe. At any rate, what we are has been removed from her. What we are is what she lacks. And when we sleep we sleep her sleep. No sooner had Maria stepped into the room than she turned on her heels and crept off to the piano room. Slaked her breakfast-hot-chocolate-thirst by hammering out Bach on the piano. Until something suddenly loomed close. Stole into her nostrils. She was so taken aback that she broke off from playing.

The Kornmann boy was standing beside her, saying he'd saved the cup of hot chocolate for her. How could she possibly thank him? Either for the chocolate or the discovery it had led to. Evidently her nose was beginning to work again.

She is secure up here. Ossine will not come up this far. She will not go up what she cannot count, Maria thought. The disadvantage: too many stairs between Maria and her piano. Although having studied the way up and down closely she can now get downstairs quickly. And back up again. Playing the piano she almost forgot the time. Mesmer's visit! She only remembered because Kaline reminded her. She can still make it. So, dash back up the stairs. Two at a time. Half-way up she was out of puff. Paused for breath on the landing where the staircase gets tighter. The remaining stairs narrow and steep. When she arrived at the top she could already hear the doctor making his way up. His heavy, regular footsteps. Always in rhythm. No pauses, no stopping to catch his breath. Nothing detains him. He walks as he breathes. Powerfully. A velvety power. This is how she imagines the moon, which he talks about so often. The moon and the sea. Powers beyond measure. He has got to the bottom of them. And he shares his knowledge with her. With Maria.

The dog came trotting in with Mesmer. It would not have come on its own, she thought. It stood beside her, panting, nudging her hands with its wet nose. Straight away she tried to smell it and couldn't help laughing. She'd have liked to feel his nose, slowly and thoroughly, with both hands. But this dog's nose will not keep still, no matter how tenderly she caresses it.

Stroking hands, no thank you. The dog's muzzle darts out of the way at once. For her, however, hands filled with hidden objects are irresistible. And to find what's hidden seems to her to be the meaning of life.

Maria had Kaline bring up a jar of water which always had to be full. This attracts the dog, too. She kept on sniffing the water until the tip of her nose felt wet. How delicate smells are in comparison to light. So delicate that she would not be able to find water. The dog would. In the dark as well as the light.

Mesmer said he'd brought her something. A surprise. And she had run over to him, her arms outstretched. To receive the something. He took it away. From under her nose, from her grasp. And she felt tricked. Thought he shouldn't have done that. She wanted to give it a sniff at least. She could have howled. He took off her blindfold. Said: Come on, be brave, when she didn't dare open her eyes. It was dark in the room, he said. Too dark to hurt. So open those eyes. Think of the empress.

What did the empress have to do with it? Why bring the empress into everything? Into everything heroic.

What was heroic about opening one's eyes? he wanted to know. It was true that Kepler said light rays were the equivalent of the spirit in the animal body. But she shouldn't misunderstand this. Light was not a wild animal, he said.

But it feels like it, she said. Like a wild animal in pursuit of her eyes. And unfamiliar.

Well, he said. That means I'm the animal tamer then. Your very own personal light tamer. He was at her service. For her alone. When he says things like this it makes her laugh. When she laughs nothing hurts.

She opened her eyes, waited for the pain. And waited in vain. Noticed that the doctor was waiting for something, too. Also in vain. She could not help him with whatever he was waiting for. But she could tell him that she had smelled the hot chocolate today.

She listened to him write something down. Said that smells were like birds. Thought this was a splendid phrase. And he might write it down, too.

But he said she should focus on her eyes.

She tried. Opened her eyes wide. She waited and waited, let him wait far too long, she thought. Heard the dog drinking. It was such a wet-sounding slobber that she imagined the dog to be a gushing fountain, soon this deluge of water would wash them all down the stairs. She burst out laughing.

What's so funny? he said.

Nothing, she said, turning to him and saying: Yes, something was different from usual. She could feel something fluttering through her eyes, through the light tubes, she said, like the arrival of a gentle breeze. At the same time something in her head was pulling to the back with all its might. A sensation like her eyes being torn off. What that was, she couldn't say.

Sounds like progress. Mesmer took her hand and, as if that were not reward enough, led her to the thing. She guessed what the sphere was at once. A globe! He guided her fingers across America where, as she knew, Indians lived. Then her fingers wandered across the globe of their own accord. Surely Cape Horn must stick out somewhere. She pressed her body to the object. Felt pleased to be embracing the entire world. Why had the doctor brought her a world? She thought he had something in mind for her. She sensed it. Was looking forward to it. Just didn't know what it was.

Was she crying? he said, and she wiped away a tear, shrugged her shoulders and started to laugh. The globe smelled so dry.

Mesmer took her finger and led it half-way round the sphere. Here, he said. We're right here. You and I. And right here is where you will learn how to see.

The following day it was his telescope that she recognized, not with her eyes but with her fingers. First a globe, now the telescope, she thought. With a telescope, her geography tutor had said, it was now possible to do what only magicians had been capable of in the past. The stars could be brought down to earth. Everything far away could be brought down. The telescope transformed distance into proximity. It had taken her a little while to grasp that people were unable to understand the things they brought down to earth. That was precisely what was magical about it. And today? What did he have today?

Something magnificent, he says.

She hears him place the object on the table.

Today, he says, we're going to play "No touching". And today we're going to stick to the rules.

We? she says.

He hesitates. You, he says.

Me? she says. What about you?

Me, he says.

I understand, she says. Is it something else from his laboratory? Another magic device?

First, he says, there are no magic devices lying around in my laboratory, only scientific instruments. Second, she should look, not guess.

As usual she stretches out her arms. He stands behind her, reaching under her armpits for her hands. Gently pulls her arms back to her body. She thinks she can smell him, and he smells like pepper tastes. Reason enough to stretch her arms out again.

Eyes open, he says.

Having her hands against her body and not being allowed to touch anything is like having had them amputated. Like the wounded on the battlefields of Kalin and Olmütz that the count told her about. Limbs shot through beyond remedy. They screamed even before the amputation. They screamed the moment they regained consciousness. Has he ever amputated hands? she says.

What makes her think that? Her hands are not comparable to those of soldiers, he says. Soldiers have war hands. Yours are made of gold.

Like yours, she says.

Would the empress invest otherwise?

I'm sure she would, Maria says. The empress had to stand up to Prussia. She could do with every single hand for the war. Gold or not. Anyway, her father said that the empress now prefers music to war.

Who doesn't? he says. Now open your eyes, please.

Not until he tells her how it's done. Amputating a hand. With a saw.

Had he ever done that?

Alright then, he says. Yes. And her eyes had much to learn, he says. So: Look! What's on the table?

She does want to, but she cannot stick by the rules of the game. Her arms stick out as if independent of her body. And he, with his wonderfully warm hands, pulls them back again.

This pointless opening of the eyes! Why is he torturing her? Cretin.

Waste of time, she says. She doesn't know.

Get closer, he says.

Why can't she touch it? Just briefly. For a second. Was he trying her patience?

No, he says. You mine? Open your eyes.

114

Repeating it won't make a difference.

Can she see anything?

How should she know?

What's over there?

No idea. Something.

Dark and light? Lighter and darker?

She wasn't a parrot. So she'd prefer it if he kept quiet, she says. Adding, there's no way she can touch it.

What? he says. What can't she touch.

She calls it *areas*. She can't touch the *areas*.

Patches, he says. Congratulations, he says. You're seeing patches. Light and dark.

The third significant progress in his treatment, he notes. As a reward she's allowed to reach out and touch the patches.

She could have given him a slap. But there's nothing there.

She thrashes around with her hands. Nothing. Just thin air. She stumbles. Falls over. Sits up.

Now she suddenly can't feel her face any more either.

Don't worry, it'll soon pass, he says, pulling her up.

He's like her father. He doesn't take her seriously. Not one bit. Her face starts twitching. In the same old sequence. Eyes, cheeks, mouth, arms, legs. She feels like smashing everything to bits. Especially Doctor Mesmer. The things he calls patches are starting to burn. Burn and itch. Closing her eyes doesn't help. Her hands don't help. Nothing helps. Throwing herself on the ground, howling.

This is a waste of her time, she says. If only everybody could see as she does. It's not normal. She says he's taught her enough. Enough is enough.

When he doesn't say anything, she shouts that he should leave her in peace. Disappear. Out of her life. She wants to stay as she is.

It's too late, he says, for that. She's changed already. He knows it. She knows it. And soon the whole world will.

No, she shouts.

So why are her eyes no longer bulging? And why is she suddenly describing smells?

Fine, she says, he's right. Her eyes have changed. And her nose. She doesn't need anything else. Why should she want to change at all? Why's he insisting on it?

He's not insisting she change.

She's content. With herself. Her life. Seeing, why bother? I can play piano without it.

Now *she's* sounding like her father, he says.

Horrified, she turns her head towards him.

Alright then, he says, wrapping the blindfold around her.

He takes it back. The magnificent, unknown object. As a punishment. She'd hoped it would stay there. She would have thrown herself on top of it. Feeling and sniffing it as and when she wanted. It's what she fancied doing right now. She might have crushed it. Smashed it to smithereens. Flung it down those stairs she's running down now, to the piano, where else? To get this magnificent, unknown object out of her head at last.

She removes the blindfold, blinks at the keyboard. Third movement of the Haydn concerto. A rondo. More precisely, the first ten bars. When she makes a mistake she repeats the passage. She is making lots of mistakes today. More than usual.

She concentrates on the tricky bits. The entire afternoon consists of tricky bits. It sounds like Kaline chopping onions. But this is a rondo! It should breathe lightness. Inaudible finger changes. Her fingers are not working.

Stop for today. Stop, before she takes even more steps backwards.

Be wary of today. There are days when the wolf gets its revenge. It attempts to destroy, devour everything one has worked hard for over many lamb-like days. She must keep herself safe. In a peaceful place. And where is it more peaceful than where the pigeons live?

Silence in her room. An unfamiliar silence. A pregnant silence. Where are the pigeons? She stops. Not even sleeping pigeons? It's probably later than she thinks. Are those patches or is she mistaken? The patches seem reliable. That at least. Reliable in their restless flickering and quivering. Like herself. She wraps the blindfold around her head again. Imagines she's finished looking after her eyes, put them to bed. As the nurse once used to put her to bed. Now she can relax, Maria and her eyes. A comfortable doze in the armchair. Let the day pass by from the safety of this height.

There's a rustling in the room. A pigeon that's strayed inside? The rustling doesn't sound like feathers.

Hello? Maria says, and gets a rustle for an answer. The one familiar piece in this puzzle is the soft, muffled ringing. She approaches the noise. A ringing and rustling fly away from her. The moment she moves, they move too. If she stands still, the noises stop.

She pauses. Starts humming, lowers her head. Strikes out

suddenly. Arms out to the front as if playing Blind Man's Buff. On her hunt through the room Maria catches a dress, a woman. She digs her fingers into her prey.

Ow! Kaline says. Ow! and Sorry!

How familiar–unfamiliar this feels: Maria's dress. Kaline's body. Maria's wig. Kaline's neck. Her chin, her ears. Kaline's earlobes. Maria's earrings dangling from them. Kaline's firm forearms, her soft *décolleté* and a little too much dress for too little bust and these unfamiliar transitions between taffeta and skin and lace and fluffy hair!

She's so terribly sorry.

All Maria can think of is: What on earth was she thinking of?

Kaline! Cheat. Thief. Take it off. Right away. This place is swarming with cretins. She's sick of them . . .

She just wanted to see, Kaline says, what a dress like that would . . .

Just wanted to see? Maria screams, you're clearly a total imbecile.

She hears Kaline getting undressed. The clothes comes off, layer by layer, each one placed in a pile before the next is removed. Taffeta dress, corset, bodice. First petticoat, second petticoat. Ending with Kaline, naked, the tower of a hairpiece on her head. What a muffled sound. In contrast to the hairpins which ring out as they clatter one by one on the table.

I'm sorry, Kaline mutters. If she'd known how badly the young lady would take it she'd have had shown some self-control.

Control? Maria shouts as Kaline gets into her own clothes

which sound like empty potato sacks you throw on a heap for burning. How on earth can she know what that is? Other people have total control over her.

Oh, the young lady sounds so learned when she speaks, Kaline says. She's awfully smart. And surely she understands that the doctor mustn't find out about this. What he finds out, his wife finds out. You don't need to be smart to know what, even if you don't know how. Please, she'll lose her job otherwise.

It's your own fault, Maria yells, starting to cry.

Saying no more, Kaline joins in.

Two women on the bed, crying their eyes out, starting to comfort each other.

To say something nice, Maria says she envies Kaline. Kaline can see.

It's not easy. And the young lady's the one to envy. She's so talented. I can't do anything, she says. And of all the things she can't do, the one she misses most of all is reading. Not being able to read is like not being able to walk. She has to rely on people reading to her.

But it's the same for Maria. She can only read with Pestalozzi's board. Otherwise she relies on help. And in her case that meant her father. Who helps you, she says?

Mmm, Kaline says. My father can't read.

Who then?

She can't say. Secret.

I'll keep it to myself, Maria says.

Sure?

You have my word.

It would all be over if it came out!

What would be over? Maria says.

Everything.

It's all over anyway. Maria laughs when Kaline winces.
Tell me, who? The doctor? A patient? Who?

Him, Kaline says. Every night. When the household is asleep.
Who?

No, she's not going to say, Kaline says. Only that once he
asked for hot milk late at night. Because of him she spends half
the night in the kitchen. No sooner had she brought the milk
than he said she should put it on the table. Then he suddenly
closed the door. From the inside. He told her to make herself
comfortable.

And, did she? Maria says.

First she went to the door. But he took hold of her wrist.
Led her to the armchair. She was reluctant, but sat down.
Kaline giggles. Why not? He read to her from a well-known
book. How thrilling! The only problem was that she was
hooked straight away. She'd spend the entire day thinking of
the cosy evenings, of the young lady in the book. She always
wore such fine clothes. And so that's why she just wanted to
see what . . .

What was the book called?

Don't know. A love story. From real life. Not hers.

Her father read to her from the bible, Maria says. She
knows it practically by heart. And Gellert and some Klopstock.
But he gave real life as wide a berth as you would to plague-
stricken houses. So for that she relied on her friends and visits
to the opera.

Did she want to know another secret? Kaline says.

She was still waiting for the first one. Even though she could guess.

What?

The count, Maria says.

How did she work it out?

It's obvious, Maria says. It's always the count. In every opera, in every novel it's the count.

She had to go. Kaline gets up. She's still got a lot to get through. It's got to be done. She doesn't want to jeopardize her one hour. She's so curious.

She adjusts her clothes.

No, she says, heading for the door. It's more than curiosity. It's like learning to walk . . . or see.

I understand, Maria says.

Kaline goes down the stairs slowly and uncertainly. She has left the door open so that Maria can call out after her.

Did Kaline by any chance bump into the doctor this lunchtime? When he was coming down the stairs after his visit?

Yes, why?

Was he holding anything?

Hold on, Kaline says. He might have been.

What was it?

Looked heavy. It was wrapped in a white cloth. He took it to his laboratory. Why was she asking?

⤙ CHAPTER TEN ⤚

21 March, 1777

Tomorrow is going to be a big day. The climax of his therapy. He's going to expose her eyes. Will ask her to keep them closed. He will stand before her. In his purple suit. The white stockings held up by white ribbons. He will instruct her to point her head towards his voice and open her eyes. She will obey him as she always obeys. She will look at him. Him. Her person.

The preparations are coming along. Since lunchtime a hammering of wood has been resounding throughout the house. The coachman, on Mesmer's orders, is removing the last pieces of timber from the windows in the little attic room. Not only can the young lady tolerate light now, she needs it. Without fail. And in the right doses.

The noise penetrates all the way to the magnetic baquet. Riedinger tries in vain to blanket it out for the doctor and patients with his Bach solo. Should he, Mesmer, have lent a hand? He ought at the very least to have known that it would take a coachman more than half a day to remove the timbers. That's probably why he'd looked so embarrassed and said, I'm a coachman after all. And I'm a doctor, Mesmer had replied. At which the other man had set about his work without another word.

Anna knew it. She has fled. She's with the dressmaker. Time to splash out at her leisure. He'll be delighted. He'll have the opportunity to tailor the very latest items for her. Top quality from Paris. As expensive as they are unnecessary.

Whatever the coachman does, he does properly. If he hammers, he does it properly. And if the wood splinters beneath his hammer, then it does so properly. It sounds as if he's chopping enough wood to last the winter. But all he is doing is taking a few nails from the timbers. Nails which have sat in this wood for longer than Mesmer has been living here. Who knows who first nailed up the windows. Probably the lieutenant-colonel from the supply bureau. On account of the window tax. This man has entered his thoughts far too often recently. When she talks about the past Anna shows as little restraint as when she's out shopping. When Mesmer thinks of all he's learned about the lieutenant-colonel from the supply bureau. Far more than necessary. That he was an excellent horseman – that much was fine. That he could speak English, French, Greek and Russian. That he liked hunting. That he aimed and shot and never missed. That would have been enough. Taken together with the portrait by the fireplace, Mesmer could have put together a picture of a tolerable predecessor. A worthy one. Anna didn't have to tell him, however, that the lieutenant-colonel frequently had bad breath. He was forced to register this as a medical statement. But the fact that the lieutenant-colonel liked kissing nonetheless, more specifically sticking his tongue deep into Anna's mouth, how was a man to classify information like that? She could have kept it to herself. Especially as it compromised all the more harmless comments. But obviously her mouth needed to come out with it. And now Mesmer is fighting a running battle with a phantasm. One which is forever flashing through his mind. Whenever he looks at her mouth. Or when he's feeling weak. And it prevents him from probing more deeply into Anna's past life. From asking, for example, whether the lieutenant-colonel could have driven a nail into a wooden bar. He would have been interested in knowing this now. And whether he could have taken the nails out himself. Or would he have got the coachman to do it, too?

But where are his thoughts leading him? He needs to concentrate. Like his patients, who are desperately trying to sway in harmony. Impossible with this racket. Even the slightest noise causes convulsions in our neural pathways. Each change of sound, each beat is reflected in the patients. Let alone a hammer blow. Even though Riedinger is trying his best. He's finished the Bach, now he's marching, a little too hammer-like, through a sweet little tune. Why doesn't he play a march? Why doesn't he square up to the hammering with a march? This dainty little piece! The patients are clearly beside themselves. The young lady holds her iron rod now to her right ear, now to her left. The count is resting his forehead on it, as if all were lost. There's not one who isn't moving the rod somewhere around their head. Mistress Ossine is abusing her skull. And poor old Riedinger is chasing through a nervous, far too rapid *andantino affectuoso*. When the doorbell joins in as a third voice, once, twice, three times, it's clear that there will be no more harmony.

Either Kaline can't hear anything or doesn't want to. Or has she vanished? Taken flight with the pigeons. At the moment he doesn't have the imagination to reflect on where.

Mesmer, the door opener, leaves his patients at the baquet to let in a young man. Who, above the hammering, wishes him good-day, as if this were the purpose of his visit. And hands him a letter from the Imperial–Royal chancellery. No eyes are needed to tell this. You can feel it by the paper.

Finally. Finally the court secretary has disclosed to the empress what soon everybody in Vienna will be talking about. The new method, the method that cures. Discovered by him, Mesmer, who searched and searched. Until God granted that he should find.

The letter which will be the watershed in his life. Dividing it into the bleak past and successful future. A life of which the empress knows nothing, and the life of the empress, in his name. The life in the shade, the life in the sun. *Ante* and *post*. On that side. On this side. Breathe out, hold and . . . breathe in. It's his old life from which he looks at the blond messenger of the gods. The bringer of a dazzling future. While his hands unfold the paper. Is it not true that special news is brought by special messengers? Who look like princes, sons of the light. Regular teeth, snow-white cuffs. The long, tied-back hair beneath a fur cap. And outside, a white stallion glistening with sweat.

But Herr Paradis keeps it short. His dispatch dispatches the disappointed Mesmer so firmly back to his old life that all thoughts of a new one perish at a stroke. To be precise, the letter does nothing more than confirm what he already knows.

Tomorrow, early tomorrow morning, the court secretary will pay a visit to see the progress his daughter is making. Yours sincerely. With an outsized sepia signature, bloody at the edges, and a few blots. Nothing more. The measure of all things. The court secretary. No empress, no patient, no doctor.

He'll do everything possible to prevent Herr and Frau Paradis from simply turning up here and throwing his therapy programme and timetable into chaos. When he looks at the messenger a second time, Mesmer notices that the man's at least half a head taller than himself. How snootily he's smiling down at him. No, he's smirking. And he smells. A foul stench under the lemon water.

Mesmer has him wait outside the laboratory. He'll take the reply back to his master right away.

So now he has to write a letter, too. As if it weren't enough to have patients waiting at the baquet and Riedinger fiddling against a coachman who's giving the house such a shake that Kaline has sought to escape with the pigeons.

Tomorrow impossible, he writes, underlining both words. But it's not enough. People expect him to give reasons. That's the biggest nuisance. The need to give reasons. He starts at the beginning.

On no account should there be any interruptions to the process in which his daughter is making clear progress. He requests their patience, he writes. I need this one extra day.

Alone with your daughter. She now knows what's expected of her. She knows what's at stake. She does what she's told. I am amazed. And you. You will be amazed. At how the girl concentrates. On everything put before her. How she tries to see. And how she can look. You won't recognize her! She can make out objects. The globe on the table. The telescope and the fortepiano. The microscope. Tomes in the library. Her wig. The wig stand and whatever is put before her.

The father should not be worried by the lack of people in this list. People, the climax of this story, will be the next stage. I am expecting much of this, Mesmer writes. I? He crosses out the I. Writes a You above it. Gadzooks. Now he's got to write the whole thing again.

Maria looks forward to being with people. She's curious. About herself, too. Tomorrow is the day. His big day. Her big day. A big day for both of them.

He, Mesmer, will be the first. The first she sets her eyes on. The first she will know. He can't let something like that be ruined by an impatient father.

The windows are being liberated at this very moment. Light can once again enter this tiny room which has been darkened for years. Mesmer crosses out the sentence. He crumples up the letter, goes to the door. The messenger has vanished. Instead there is Kaline. Audibly at least. Her inviting, high-pitched girl's laughter resonates in-between the hammer and violin. Mesmer's instinct tells him that he only needs to follow the laughter to find the messenger. The laughter leads him to the kitchen. Where the messenger is leaning against the doorframe, exchanging glances and being rewarded for every word. Each hint of a sign, each attempt at a gesture is rewarded by her sparkling laughter.

Tell Herr Paradis, Mesmer interrupts, that alas I'm indisposed tomorrow. One day later, on the other hand, the day after tomorrow, he'll be happy to expect him in the morning. Enough. He has things to do. A messenger may be able to stand around keeping other people from their work. Not a doctor. And certainly not a housemaid, he wants to add, but stops himself, after Kaline first looks at him angrily, then beseechingly, then lowers her head in anticipation, reaching into her apron and taking out a letter which she hands him.

It was brought by the messenger who came to fetch the Kornmann boy this morning.

Fetch?

Kaline doesn't need to know how much of a surprise this is for him.

The first thing he does when back in his room is read Banker Kornmann's note of thanks. Mesmer has saved the most precious thing in his possession, his dear son. He regrets he was unable to come to Vienna in person to pick up the boy. This time there was no external reason. Rather it was turmoil in his most inner circle, his family, which made the journey impossible. He was sending his servant, his most loyal one. In the coupé, his fastest. Pulled by his most tireless horses. To bring Benjamin home. With the most heartfelt gratitude.

He reads it once. Twice. Three times . . .

23 March, 1777

It is silent in the house. The coachman has done good work. The result is enthusiasm, and it even convinces Mesmer. In spite of its small windows the tiny attic room is lighter than those on the floor below. A perfectly adequate room.

How high up you are here. And how far you can see. Across the entire sky. And half the earth. All the way to the Prater. Where he can see himself playing as a child. The coachman's voice almost cracks. But he's pessimistic about the pigeons. The pigeons will be back. And move up here. He knows pigeons. They can't be driven away. But he'll come up with something. What the coachman comes up with will be good. Rome isn't lost, and the attic room hasn't fallen to the pigeons' claws.

She's ready and he's standing in front of her. Standing as he always does, dressed in purple satin, steady, solemn. Wipes a dog hair from his sleeve. Hums softly. Watches her raise her head slightly. As if she were picking up a scent.

Gigantic, she says. If she didn't find repetition pointless she'd add that he was overbearing.

Why isn't she sticking to their agreement? She shouldn't be looking yet.

She is sticking to it, she says. Her eyes are closed. Look how closed my eyes are.

Then please stop guessing, he says.

She's not guessing.

So how does she know?

Know what?

That he's overbearing.

She can sense it. And hear it. What a tenor!

He's heard often enough that he has a big voice. Also that purple is his colour. From his mother, the priest, patients. Later on from Anna. At some point he adopted the views others had of him. At some point he took on their opinions. He learned to see through his mother's eyes. This tiny, rather delicate woman who's only ever been offhand with him. But offhand only because she was ashamed of being proud of him. Franz Anton. One metre seventy-two. Compact. Neither thin nor fat. A precisely measured giant. Who can do everything, pray, sing, swim. And arithmetic. He can draw, too. And hunt. The list is endless. Teachers flounder in the presence of such talent. And he saw the glint in her eyes. The pride. And how the seed of this onset of affection germinated into anger, jutting her chin forward, jamming her lower teeth in front of the upper set. She looked like a bulldog. And the same face when she held the cat in her lap. Affection at first, then she fondled it roughly. Ruffling its hair as she clutched it tightly. Like the cat, Mesmer was wary of her affection. Which was gentle to start with. And violent in the end. How strong he was, she would say. And handsome. Well-built. How stable and reliable. She would slap him on the back with such force, as if she were trying to fell like a Christmas tree the stability she cherished.

His wife Anna also waxes lyrical about his strength. Sometimes she clings on to his arm. Rests her head on his shoulder. He only needs to flex his biceps and she wants to kiss him. There and then. On more than just the mouth.

Maria's face remains relaxed. Where he's standing her hands cannot touch him. Not even if she stretches out her arms.

He starts moving. Swings his hips. Shifts his weight from one leg to the other. Raises his arms, his hands in white gloves. Tracing arabesques in the air. Like the oriental dancer in Rome that Messerschmidt talked about. This is how he dances. As if to the slowest music.

Open your eyes. He says.

She obeys.

For the first time he can see her looking at him. Her gaze resting on him. And her head following the eyes. In minuscule, echo-like movements. And how absolute her attention. And how she's striving to banish all thoughts of what was and what will be. He can see that she's striving to see. He makes a mental note that she imagines her perception depends on the degree of her concentration.

She doesn't say anything. What is there to say?

He begins to turn around. Slowly, imperceptibly like the earth.

She keeps her head still, blinking. For some time. She grants him a whole period of silence.

Oh God! How terrible! she then says. She turns away. Her hands spring to her face.

Is she feeling pain?

She stiffens. Is seized by a spasm. Is she crying? He goes over to her. No, thank God. She's not crying. But what . . . He pauses. Watches her blinking through her fingers. Another spasm.

Too much of a good thing? He wants to know. Will she . . .

Her body shakes. She cannot speak. She laughs. Shudders with laughter.

When she sees me, he notes, her nerves react with sheer overexcitement.

What's so funny? he says.

He waits. For her to calm down.

No . . . Just . . . that thing there.

What does she mean?

That . . . that disgusting thing over there, she says . . . there . . . on your face.

That's my nose.

A silent fit of laughter which convulses her body.

I'm sorry. It looks so strange, dangerous, she says, and funny, this nose . . . as if it's threatening me. As if it wanted to put my eyes out. She doubles up. Kneels on the floor. Thrusts her outstretched arms between her thighs. She cannot speak or keep quiet. She sits up. Stretches her arms out towards him. Towards his nose.

He takes a pace towards her.

For God's sake! She backs away. He should stay where he is! He'll stab her with that thing of his.

Scarcely has he moved before she's laughing. And laughing. Can hardly breathe. The laughter takes on a life of its own. Without air, he notes, and without there being anything

132

to laugh about. What should he call it? A subterranean earth-
quake, an avalanche. A hysterical force from the bright sky of
dark nature.

She's fighting for air. He calls for help from the dog which
is pretending to be asleep under the table.

She quietens down in an instant. Beckons the black beast
with her hands and sweetest, high-pitched tones. Come on.
She clicks her tongue. Come here you little devil.

She holds out a closed fist, lets him sniff it. Opens her hand
to stroke him. When he makes to go away, to Mesmer, she
holds him by the collar.

Stay, you stubborn beast. And then: I think dogs are more
beautiful than people. By their noses alone. This dog and she
go together well. She suits its face. Better than Mesmer does
Mesmer's own. Does he know what she's talking about?

Well . . . he says. Basically. Perhaps. And: Congratulations!
He could embrace her, embrace himself. He's done it.
Congratulations.
He repeats himself.
It was the condition of a moment like this, he says, watch-
ing him looking at her.
She did it, he says.
How did he know that?
He can see.
Well he can see more than her, then.
That was natural. She shouldn't worry about it. It had
nothing to do with her eyes. And: Your parents are coming
tomorrow.
Tomorrow, she says. Oh my God. Tomorrow. Already.

That's quick.

Yes, he says. He hadn't expected it to be so soon, either.

Does she have to leave here, then?

Not at all, he says. This was now the third breakthrough. And by no means the third most significant. Even though what was in store for her now was no bed of roses. She'd already taken the important steps.

And the little ones?

Her eyes were capable of anything, he says. But first they have to learn how to see again. They have to animate themselves. They have to exercise their muscles. He's very happy to help, but some things depended on her.

Help, she says. What else?

For most people, the fact that she can see will be something extraordinary. Something akin to a miracle. And as far as he can work out, there'll be lots of people wanting to see her. To satisfy themselves with their own eyes that she can see.

Could people see that from looking at her? she says.

Don't be scared, he says. It takes more than muscle power to see the world so it recognizes you.

He's making her afraid now, she says, even though she knows he's trying to achieve the opposite.

Afraid? he says. The dark fear of the light? Or the blinding fear of the dark?

⊰ CHAPTER ELEVEN ⊱

28 March, 1777

⊰∙∙⊱

They believe that concentration and silence are one and the same, but they're mistaken.

They breathe. Clear their throats. Chairs and sofas creak and groan under their shifting weight. Even when they just sit there, the dresses and wigs they're covered with rustle. And where they're uncovered they have hands, ears, eyes. Their insatiable eyes focused on her, Maria.

The advances of the past week have brought nothing but backward steps. At the piano. When practising. Haydn. Koželuh or Bach. Handel, Mozart, Salieri. Scales.

She got started, she'd told Mesmer, and all of a sudden didn't have enough fingers. When she put her hands in front of her, she found all ten of them in perfect working order and caressed them all delicately. When she stroked the dog all ten fingers were there, too. But when she had a go at Haydn, she could only find three fingers on her left hand plus her thumb. And with her right she could barely manage the triplets in the second movement. When she came to the sextuplets, finding herself with only seven small fingers, she failed miserably each time, as she already had with the demisemiquavers in the first movement.

Mesmer advised her to continue playing. With open eyes, open ears and an open heart. In peace.

She did. Played with open eyes and open ears until her heart tensed up with all the dissonance. Once again her fingers charged ahead hopefully and once again toppled over each other like a troop of coach horses trying to go their separate ways. It sounded pitiful, too. In spite of all her technique.

Which of her many specialists should she turn to now?

Carl Phillip Emanuel Bach doesn't say a word about it in his Piano School.

She turned to Riedinger.

He said he knew all about those times when nothing seemed to go right. She shouldn't feel disheartened. She was a musician to her very core, he said. That would never change.

This made her feel so much better that she dared ask him whether he might help her with her composition. She had so much music in her head, she said, and it was torture to be unable to write anything down.

He agreed straight away.

Mesmer had little more to say about her problem, and nothing that might have helped. Phrases such as: Don't worry about making mistakes. Don't worry if you falter. It'll soon get better.

And if it doesn't?

Not important.

So pray, what is important?

That you can see.

She didn't want to see anything. She wanted to play. She put on the blindfold. Her finger problem wasn't going to disappear that quickly and all by itself. If she plays the Haydn her fingers will start playing up. She'll make mistakes. Just as she's been making mistakes all week, all day long. Not just at the piano.

His impatience as soon as her father kissed her forehead. How fleeting the contact. How quickly he moved away again. As did the mother. As if their kisses were not serious. By contrast, the question of why Maria's eyes were blindfolded, why the most important things had been kept secret from them, the parents, that was serious. So serious that the doctor affected an excessive cheerfulness to avoid having to start the day with these two looking dumbfounded.

You can't play around with light, he declared, as if there were nothing more plausible to say. It had to be given in the right doses. Precise doses. Otherwise it would do more harm than good.

Where's your beautiful wig? the mother asked.

She'd discarded it, Maria said. She spoke softly as if she were unsure.

This emboldened her mother to utter a loud and clear: But why?

Because it's monstrous.

And what did she call that thing on her head . . . The mother was at a loss to find a description.

Not the father . . . hacked stubblefield, he said . . . this hail-ravaged vineyard. A gruesome sight. Couldn't it be covered up, just for his sake?

And Kaline scurried out and back in again, and on her cheek Maria felt the silk cloth like a draught of air before Kaline tied it around her head.

That's a bit better, the father said sounding distressed, but with a hint of excitement.

She knows this. Whenever he feels aggrieved his voice signals the wish for instant redress, an instant distraction, preferably music.

What are you going to play for us? he says, although he already knows.

I'm going to play the Haydn concerto, she hears herself say.

Oh, he says, really?

Yes, she hears herself say, Haydn.

And she thinks of the handful of snow which she'd recently shaped into a perfect ball. A reflection of her sheer delight in the winter and the melting sensation in her hands. She'd rolled the ball through the snowy garden until it became taller and heavier than herself. A massive, deformed lump that could no longer be shifted from where it stood.

All three movements, she says. And doesn't believe it. Not a single word. Believes what she hears herself not saying. I can't play now. Something has changed. Within me. Haven't a clue what. Something between my fingers and eyes and ears. A sort of reconfiguration. My hands are working. My ears. My eyes. But nothing adds up. One thing subtracts from another. And there's nothing left.

Apart from fear. And fear of this fear. And trembling hands. Smiles and silence. Ridiculed, dishonest. That's her.

It was a mistake to tell her parents why she's not wearing the wig.

The wig makes her head small. As small as a pea beneath a mountain of dusty feathers. Why hadn't anybody told her?

Because it's not true, her mother said.

So what? her father said, wanting to know how she'd arrived at this conclusion.

She said she'd sat in front of the mirror. Rather a long time, she said. And rather an intensive time. They'd become friends. The mirror, the reflection and her.

That was a mistake. Her father despises mirrors.

They'd barely let their daughter out of the house and she was sinning already. For many years he'd invested time and the best reading matter in her. First and foremost the book of books. And barely was she out of the house than she was letting vanity prance around her head. Did she think it was right to stare at herself in the mirror? She should stare at the keyboard, that paid dividends at least.

But he's wrong.

Mesmer had to promise to keep her away from the mirror in future. Which he did. Otherwise her father would have taken her away on the spot. She's resentful towards Mesmer for having done so, instead of defending her. As resentful as her mother was of her for not wearing the pretty bonnet.

À la Matignon. The very latest thing in Paris. Imported specially for her.

It doesn't suit me, Maria had replied.

Her mirror wisecracks suited her even less.

The father sounded as if it were the most dreadful thing she'd ever done.

As Mesmer said nothing, she had to defend herself.

I've no idea, she said, why I should wear this heavy, uncomfortable thing. There's no benefit to it. It's pointless. It's not even beautiful.

Beautiful. This made her father laugh.

Did she know what she was talking about? For her it was enough to look neat and tidy.

And her mother, who adopted his tone straight away, noticed that she was only half dressed. The bodice, which gave her hefty build a delicate form, some elegance, was missing. And where was the long train?

The train makes me sad, she'd said. She couldn't move freely in clothes like that. She felt cooped up, unable to breathe properly. How was she supposed to sing without breathing properly? She said whatever occurred to her. It wasn't enough. Until it occurred to her that perhaps this was the very problem. The now. This moment. She realized that she only ever spoke from the moment, and sensed the problem at that moment. And scarcely had the moment passed than another followed in which she sensed something else. And when she articulated it, it was gone, blown away with the draught whistling through the house, ungraspable.

There's no system, she thought, making everything solid.

Someone to keep hold of it? She's missing her friends.

What she was saying was baseless. No hand, no foot to give it a foundation. So shaky that her parents could easily knock it down and stamp all over it.

What nonsense, the mother said. What made her say such a thing? She'd always sung so beautifully up to now.

What actually *was* wrong with her?

The father sounded as if he was refusing to take her seriously at all.

Nothing, she said.

She wasn't sure that was the right answer. Because it gave rise to a gaping silence. Into which Maria, to prevent it getting any bigger, said: But I don't want to be sad. Silence.

Then a suggestion which rescued the situation: Let's go for a walk. In the garden. It's such a nice day, the air outside is wonderful.

Her mother was immediately keen. The father rejected it all. The garden, the cold, the wet and the muddy ground. The dirt and the mother who'd immediately embraced Maria's suggestion.

He called the suggestion a fit of desperation and blamed it on her affectations. Which should be allowed to vent themselves at the piano rather than in the garden. That's where they were most tolerable. Able to be translated into something useful. Possibly. Dear Resi.

She'd nodded. The key was to not arouse any mistrust, any suspicion.

Had she been practising assiduously?

Every day.

That was the saving grace. She had to spin time into gold.

Time passes. But you can only do what you can do. And nobody can take any more from you.

Oh, if only he were right in everything, he said.

There were plenty of others, he said, who were good. Last week the Martinez girl played for the empress.

And? Maria asked.

Well, he said. You couldn't deny she had the three Ts. Temperament, technique and talent. But you, he added softly, you've got at least four. Because your name is Theresia. You're better. If you want to be.

Thank God the mother insisted on a combination of springtime and air. The doctor, too, when he finally opened his mouth recommended they start in the garden. They were right, the two of them.

Wrap up warm, they said, and get out into the sunshine.

Afterwards he'd take her blindfold off, Mesmer promised.

He probably thought the day would be salvaged. As soon as he showed the parents Maria's eyes. How quickly he was talking to the father all of a sudden. He was smoothing things over. Without the father's noticing. He was too far away for that. Somewhere, God only knew, in his Imperial–Royal world. Of chamber music concerts, church, chamberlains, Chancellor Kaunitz and his cherished empress.

Then, suddenly, he'd stood in front of Maria, as if he were trying to prevent her from going outside.

He raised his hand, said: Stop! He wanted to see her eyes now. This minute. Otherwise he wouldn't come outside with them.

She'd refused. That was the doctor's decision.

And the doctor decided. He gave in. Took off her blindfold.

No! No, I don't believe it, she heard her father say. Resi! Eyes like . . .

He'd scurried around her.

Say something too, he snapped at the mother.

She obeyed. Eyes . . . like pigeons' hearts . . .

What a comparison, he'd laughed.

. . . concealed in feathers . . .

That was the most irrelevant comment he'd ever heard.

Those are eyes, proud . . . like chestnuts . . . in their prickly bed . . . no, not that at all . . . eyes like . . . ships sunk in the rain.

Yes, he liked that.

How do they feel, Resi?

Fine, she'd said, smiling again as Mesmer covered up the ships with the darkness they were used to.

Smoothly.

She'd already been in the garden that morning. Very early. Ever since the song of the blackbirds had been celebrating the arrival of spring, she'd been tempted outside almost every morning. Secretly. The fact that she froze was irrelevant. It wasn't the cold air which gave her goose pimples.

But the main reason for going into that cold air: the blackbirds' voices rising to the heavens. She couldn't get enough of them. Wanted to listen up close. Miss nothing of the long, melancholic melodies which all of a sudden they would counterpoint with jubilant trills.

She could hear someone walking slowly along the gravel path below the avenue. Assuming it was Mesmer, she approached the footsteps.

Then she heard the voice. Overlaid with the voices of blackbirds. Or in conversation or competition with them. She wanted to get closer. But the moment she stepped on the gravel the blackbirds took fright, shooting in all directions and clamouring vociferously.

Mesmer had stood there.

Good morning, he said. Wasn't she cold?

They'd returned to the house together.

Her parents were in that same spot where the blackbirds had made such a fuss that morning. Her father had taken her hand. No sooner had he touched it than she also felt her mother's hand tugging at her. As if she had to be divided up fairly.

So what had she seen so far? The father sounded perky.

All sorts of things.

No, he called out. They'd heard that before.

The mother clapped her hands and snivelled. Maria put her arm around her.

Old cry baby, the father said.

The mother said that now Resi could see again, soon she probably wouldn't be needing her mother's eyes any more.

Maria heard herself disagree. The gravel crunched beneath her feet. The footsteps sounded in unison. The gravel allowed no distinction between them. As if they all thought and felt the same. And yet this was precisely what was missing that day: unity. And she, Maria, was the problem. She'd been the problem all morning.

She realizes this now.

They'd strolled along the flowerbeds, towards the Belvedere Palace.

The mother said the garden was almost like the empress's.

Rubbish, the father said. Compared to the empress's this was a dwarf garden.

Just a little smaller, the mother said, but look, it's even got an aviary and a dovecote. A disused fountain. And look, another sculpture by that F.X.M.

He told her to stop going on about that lunatic. The father felt Maria's eyes again. He couldn't believe what he'd seen.

Maria cowered.

What a strange relationship between seeing and not believing and touching.

Why not?

I'm sorry? the father said.

Why didn't he believe her?

What made her think he didn't believe her?

That's what he just said.

Sometimes you just had to understand something before believing it. Seeing on its own was not enough. First you have to have understood. At least a teeny-weeny bit of the whole.

Do you believe, she said, that what you can't understand isn't true?

No, what he meant was that eyes are sometimes dulled and stupid and can't judge anything properly.

And her mother agrees with him.

145

A teeny-weeny bit of the whole, Maria. That would be enough. She mustn't exaggerate any more.

Why was she getting involved? The father clicked his tongue.

What he'd said was purely an expression of his pleasure.

Strange, Maria said. You're pleased and yet don't believe it. Had he had many bitter experiences in his life?

Was she alluding to his time in the Banat, or what had made her come out with that?

She just thought of it.

She shouldn't go around talking so precociously, her father said. And laughed.

What about you, she said to her mother. Why don't you believe it?

Should I have a different opinion from your father? My very own?

She'd laughed. Maria joined in. Out of embarrassment. She'd been ashamed. For her mother. And when she heard the hooves of four or five horses trotting up the drive and the wheels of at least two carriages, she'd extricated herself. Had waited behind while her parents looked over to see who was arriving. While the dog barked its welcome. Maria had perched beside one of the flowerbeds. Stroked the cold blanket of snowdrops with her hand. Heard her father say: That's him. Dr von Störck. And behind him that's the other one, the cataract specialist . . . Dr Barth. Both of them. By Jove! Come, quickly.

Her mother called her name.

She fondled the cold flowers and stems more firmly. They

146

tensed under her hand. As if she were a storm. A minor, harmless storm which damages nothing. Just swooshing above the heavy, damp earth. Fondling snowdrops.

Look at your hands, Resi.

Her mother had tried to pull her up. At the word "hands" her father came over. She was sieving the earth between her fingers. Black clumps and sods slapped as they fell. Something stuck between her fingers. She wiped the dirt from it. A snail shell. Filled. Inhabited.

She tapped her fingernail against the sealed shell.

Resi! Her father screamed when she'd licked the dirt from the snail shell. Spat the saliva mixed with mud at the feet of her parents.

Shhh! You'll wake it up. With your screaming. She'll take the snail with her. The doctor has allowed her to keep it in the house. On the shelf in one of the rooms off his laboratory. With the medicinal worms. In a clay pot with a lid and air holes. A little earth instead of water, a little hay or dried leaves. Until it wakes from its winter sleep. It won't be long now. She wanted to be there when it happened.

And because she said she wanted to watch the spectacle her parents were silent.

Back in the house Kaline had helped her to clean herself before she was presented to the visitors.

A hubbub in the room when she came in. An even thicket of equally loud voices, like a thicket of small, regular branches. Where the blackbirds build their nests. She climbed in carefully, vanishing into it. Shook hands, so many that soon all of them felt the same. Her hands remained cold and she rubbed them together. She clutched a cup of hot coffee that Kaline had brought her before offering the steaming pot round.

Blending in with the voices comes from all corners the sound of the coffee being poured, which reminded her of the palace fountain. Of the rivulet running across a lower step which the birds used as a trough.

She could hear men's voices that she recognized. Other, unfamiliar voices. Doctors greeting each other with "Herr Doctor". All of them praising the sciences. One of them called the science of human beings the most useful of them all.

Unfortunately, another said, at present it was also the most incomplete.

But, the first man countered in defence, are we not discovering more every day? And he'd just read that the ancients already knew something he was observing now: that the female body seeped away faster than the male one. And that the female body wasn't as solid, but contained a greater number of loose parts. And a very soft, nasal voice which spoke of the black mutt lying around in the courtyard. What a shaggy creature! Might he borrow it? Just for an afternoon. For a new idea. A little experiment. Which might have a big impact.

And she heard Anna say the man would have to ask her husband.

From another corner a man wanted to know whether there were any electrical games on today's programme. Come on, came the answer, this is the Palais Mesmer! – So? He's got an electrostatic machine in the basement, too, hasn't he? – Yes, but, if he thought that Mesmer would be satisfied with discovering applications then he didn't know the doctor. His aims were far higher than that! The two men clinked their glasses, which rang out brightly, laughing quietly and washing down their laughter with a swig of cognac.

She could hear the delighted exclamations of her mother soar above all the other voices, commenting on the different cakes and their colours and how they matched Frau Mesmer's pale beige – or how should she describe the sublime colour of her dress, *nu, ivoire, champagne?*

And she could hear Kaline in whispered conversation with Mesmer. And Mesmer instructing her to take the dog to the laboratory immediately. And not to forget to lock the door behind her. And bring him back the key without delay.

And when her mother referred to the objects placed by Mesmer on several tables and hidden beneath white cloths as "ghosts", adding with a giggle that their daughter would now identify the ghosts for everybody, Maria knew it was time to put down her lukewarm coffee.

Her father clicked his tongue and said: In a doctor's house . . . amongst such high-class scientists . . . one doesn't talk of ghosts. Understand? And without waiting for an answer he went on: Ghosts only exist in the minds of fools.

He gave a strained laugh until at least three doctors laughed with him.

If there was anybody who believed in ghosts, he said, let them come forward. He would drive the phantasms from their head there and then, for all to see. In this house there was nothing but methods and facts.

Applause. He untied Maria's blindfold, asked if she was

ready, and when she nodded removed the first white cloth.

She turned to face the audience. The nautilus shell, she said, decorated with silver leaves and flowers.

She picked it up, pressed it to her lips and kissed it. Applause all round.

Well done, Resi! her father shouted out, very well done!

Mesmer removed one white cloth after another. There was an object below each one. And the right word from her mouth. And each word met with enthusiasm from the audience.

To finish she curtseyed, turned around, swaying slightly as she stood there blinking at the audience to the point where she felt dizzy. Everyone cheered. Her father strode forward and kissed her on the forehead.

You look fantastic. Almost as if you'd never had any treatment. She could hear Dr von Störck clearing his throat and tapped her father on the shoulder.

He went silent at once. As did everyone else. He moved his face closer to hers. She recoiled. Careful, she whispered. Your nose! She couldn't help laughing.

He called her mother.

Look at that. Do you notice anything?

Maria whipped her head to the side. What was wrong?

Nothing, nothing.

The double nothing. She gave a start. In her family this was code for red alert. Highest level of danger. Too dangerous to say.

Keep still, he said. Your mother needs a little longer.

The mother shook her head.

And he: Was she blind?

Maria could feel her mother's breath on her lips.

Can you see it yet?

Oh, her mother said, yes, I can see it.

What? he said. What can you see?

I don't know, she said.

Can't you see that Resi's eyes are different sizes?

Well, of course, she said. Now that you mention it.

Maria's face started to glow and twitch slightly.

Her father turned to Mesmer.

He was very much indebted to him.

Didn't want to diminish his achievement in any way. But look. Take a look for yourself. The right eye is smaller than the left. Would it be . . .

Is it bad? she wanted to know, but received no answer.

It will grow, Mesmer said.

Because she couldn't appear like this, her father said. Not on the international stage.

All of a sudden she felt a chubby, sweaty hand that she knew. It took her right hand and thrust it straight into the icy fingers of Dr Barth. And while the latter clasped her hand she felt the well-padded fingers of von Störck on her forehead.

Don't move, he commanded.

She strained to listen. Could hear Dr Barth whispering with Dr von Störck.

After a brief pause Störck said he must say something whether he wanted to or not.

He'd noticed it earlier, during the performance. But he hadn't wanted to interrupt the performer. Now, however, he was certain. The girl's eyes were different sizes. All the time

I treated her, he said, they were the same. The disparity had to be the result of Mesmer's therapy.

A mere trifle, Mesmer said.

Possibly, Störck said. And yet worthy of an observation, Herr Doctor.

Go and observe all you like. There's nothing more salutary than watching something disappear, Mesmer said. More important was that she had her vision back. And that this didn't disappear.

That's true, her father said. He was very much indebted to Mesmer.

He turned to Dr Störck.

What do you have to say?

He was, Störck said, very impressed. If it were really the case, he added, that the man's daughter had seen everything she named, then he was sorry that he'd taken so long to endorse the importance of this highly interesting discovery.

Dr Barth said it was bordering on a miracle. The empress had to be told of it. Right away.

Yes, but, the father said. Please wait a while with the empress. Until the trifle had disappeared.

But why? the mother said.

The father swished his arm through the air in her direction.

Mesmer said no one had two identical eyes.

He was going to check that in the mirror, the father said.

He also thought that Maria should play for the empress nonetheless. After all, when she played the empress only saw her profile. And from the side you could only see one eye. And when greeting her you bow so low that nobody can see your eyes at all. And now, he said, you're going to play for us.

And she'd sat down at the instrument while the others looked on eagerly.

She tilts her head to the audience, just slightly to show them her open eyes. Brief cheer. Then they are quiet. They think they are silence personified. They are mistaken.

Maria raises her hands.

✦ CHAPTER TWELVE ✦

12 April, 1777

A blind woman who can see again is news. Which moves faster than any change in the weather. It draws half of Vienna out onto the Landstraße and through the city gates to Mesmer's estate. (Which actually belongs to Anna.)

The sick want to be cured. The healthy beg for help, carting along their sick relatives. Others, driven by a healthy curiosity, want to see the doctor. The young lady. The miracle. The Fluid of the World.

People, horses, carriages block the courtyard, the path to the drive. There is not a patch of ground where someone is not standing or walking. Too many people for one day. Too few days for the growing masses.

Strangers burst into the magnetic baquet. Destroying the harmony. Knock on the laboratory door, tearing Mesmer away from his experiments. They knock on windows. Three times, four times, four or five knocks. As if they had to knock to check that the chaos they were causing was real. The dog can no longer tell its head from its tail. When to wag its tail, when to bark. It just stands about. Trying to do both at the same time. How stupid it looks. And how croaky it sounds. As if dejected.

Mesmer puts people off. Asks them to wait. Shoos them away. Sends them to Anna. They make appointments. And Anna takes notes. And keeps records. Everything would have fallen apart without Anna.

She anticipated it. Before the afternoon was over she was talking of success and its consequences. Saying that everything would be different now. He laughed, said she was exaggerating.

Maria had just come to the end of her painful Haydn concerto, riddled with mistakes. And he, to lift the atmosphere, had spontaneously sat at his glass instrument. Played a piece by Mozart. To relax the atmosphere. To clear the air of all wrong notes before they settle in the room, in the walls, the minds. What could be better for that than the glass armonica? Whose notes, almost visibly, swim through the room and into the furthest corners. Stretching, stretching, through the window all the way outside.

Anna, who never cries otherwise, always cries when she hears the glass armonica. And Störck, he couldn't help see this out of the corner of his eye, took her arm. Poured a glass of red for her and for himself. Disappeared out of the room with the sobbing woman and two full glasses.

When Riedinger and Hossitzky started playing dancing music he reappeared with empty glasses and a smiling Anna. Anna only danced with Störck. Störck only with Anna.

Mesmer stuck with Maria, who in spite of everything danced the minuet with a wonderful grace. She dances better than Anna. Because she's much easier to lead.

He kept Anna and Störck in his sights. The short, fat Störck and his tall, slim Anna. Towering a head above the man holding her and looking around frenziedly. She surely didn't see him, Störck or anything else. Her glances were like beacons: cast out to be seen.

He received plenty of congratulations that afternoon. On his discovery. On the successful outcome of his treatment. On the young lady who could see. Nobody was unmoved by this story. And he was congratulated on Anna. There was not a single person there who wouldn't have liked to have had a word with the hostess. And more than just one. Crowds formed wherever she was. Her in the middle. How she laughed. How crazy. Normally he spares his nearest and dearest his doctor's gaze. But now he was unable to do anything else. He saw Anna and how everything was gradually overwhelming her.

After dusk everybody gathered on the terrace. Look, Anna called out, pointing. The first sheet lightning of the year. And in a flash she had everybody's attention. She took Maria, who was happy to follow, by the hand and led her to the balustrade.

Voilà, Mademoiselle, the very first sheet lightning of your life. Enjoy it. She kissed Maria's forehead and turned her gaze to the lightning. Nobody wanted to miss this. Everyone crowded behind the two women at the balustrade.

It should have been his job to show the people there that he was showing Maria the sky. But Anna didn't seem to be aware of this. Hopefully no one else was either. She was just quicker. Quicker to get here and quicker to get away again.

At one point she was standing beside him. Her face was glowing. In the throng she grabbed his hand and squeezed it. Finally she was with him.

This was where she belonged, he whispered. At his side. She'd been much too far away from him for too long.

Don't exaggerate, she whispered. Adding something else. You did it, is what he understood. And from now on it was just a case of all their wishes coming true.

And who knew this better than Anna, engaging tirelessly in conversation with all and sundry? And while Maria, as a parting shot, was astonishing the guests by counting the stars that looked down solemnly at her, Anna let go of his hand and was instantly sucked up by the crowd.

The guests had left long ago, the residents were in their rooms, but Anna was still celebrating. She danced through the rooms as if on the shadows of notes that had faded away. He blamed it on the wine. He sat at his glass instrument. In the hope of bringing her to her senses.

She poured out two glasses of red. Full to the brim.

She had to savour his success, if he wasn't going to.

Hadn't she drunk enough already?

Enough? she said. It was a word she didn't know. Raised her glass.

What was there to savour if there was nothing from the empress, he said? The girl had played like a blind novice.

Anna thought that nobody had noticed this apart from her

father and Riedinger. They would have heard the mistakes but not registered them. Riedinger was totally besotted by the young lady. And her father had closed his eyes in delight that his daughter could now see the world with open eyes. She was getting another chance.

One, Mesmer said, was not enough. She needed lots. And an endless amount of time. So why celebrate?

He started to play. Improvised. As Haydn had advised him to when he paid a visit. Always let your imagination guide you.

The next thing he recalls is Anna throwing her arms around his neck from behind. In her newest nightdress. Which glimmers like the inside of a mussel shell. He saw the transparent material on her arms.

Dragonfly wings, cast in white sugar.

The glass instrument was dangerous, she said. The glass machine shattered your nerves. Can't you hear? she said. Those notes. Drive you mad.

Her fingertips caressed his neck.

When he failed to react she said: The glass armonica makes people sick. Melancholic. That's what Dr von Störck said.

He paused. Did she believe such nonsense?

She shook her head.

What else did he say?

Nothing. He was terribly impressed.

By what?

By a young lady cured as if it were a miracle.

Did he say that?

Yes. He compared it to a miracle.

It wasn't a miracle, he said. It was a method. He was a scientist.

The main thing was that Störck had seen that she can see. Anna shrugged her shoulders and surprised him with a satin pouch that she put into his hand.

The happier a woman, she said, the more generous she is.

Did that not mean, he said, that the more generous the more desperate? This was his experience. With women.

No, he was mistaken. She laughed at him. He might be the doctor here, but he should let her say how a woman felt.

She waited. More excited by how he would react than he by the contents of the pouch.

He had put it in his pocket.

Later, he said.

Thank God not everything's understood as it's meant.

Anna immediately thrust herself between him and the instrument. He let her.

She clasped his head. Emptied her gaze into him. That's how he felt it. Like a substance. A magnetic source.

A gaze which at that moment focused all his thoughts on Anna. Banishing everything which might distract from her. His music, his medicine, his doubts. Transforming his speechlessness into silence.

Her hand which was so agile over his body. Like the barn swallows in summer. Like shooting stars in autumn. And as light as the garlands which would soon be adorning the trees. And as delicate as the finest tendrils of the climbing vine on the wall of the house. Or a Mozart *étude*.

In contrast to her hand, Anna's gaze had weight. Pulling

their heads together like a gravitational force. While her hand fluttered about him as if detached. How different gaze and hand can be. Just as measurable substance flows over into non-measurable substance.

Without any barrier. He comes up against barriers everywhere. Closed barriers. Closed circles. The Viennese medical fraternity. Störck and his consorts. No matter how learned he was. Nor that he was a good citizen. Regularly paying his horse taxes. And sincerely offering his assistance. So long as Störck refused to endorse his method, it wasn't just hospital doors that remained closed to him. But also the doors to the Hofburg, the imperial palace.

A closed barrier. Uncertain whether it will ever be opened. Unlike the one between himself and Anna. A barrier of the sort he liked. Nothing but two long lines of contact. And which that evening loosened, blurred, dissolved. Blending into each other.

Anna dragged him onto her territory. No, that's not how it was. He'd been a willing partner for some time. A partner in crime. No, language couldn't be dragged into it on this occasion. Her slender hand which unfastened his clothes. His hand which followed her legs. Becoming caught in the rustling dragonfly wings. Wresting itself out and getting caught again. And then just Anna. The free spirit. Unapproachable Anna. So close.

He said he felt as if he were on a slippery slope. Sliding down a precipice. Unable to hold on. He only realized this was a joke when he heard her laughing.

She leapt up, adjusted her nightdress, ran out. Came back.

The night was not over yet. It was only just beginning. The darkness at the end of night. And it would last.

How right she was. The end lasted and lasted. It refused to finish. It went on and on like the notes of the glass armonica. Out through the window, across the garden, the muddy fields, the hedges, the fences and way beyond. To Vienna and further, to the Danube, to the Prater and way beyond.

While he was getting dressed the following morning the pouch dropped into his hand. Inside was a golden watch which he left where it was.

How Anna welcomes people. He hasn't taught her that. How she talks to them. And how they let her interrogate them.

And the conclusions she draws from the descriptions. About the sorts of illnesses. She wouldn't make a bad doctor. She's almost never wrong in her evaluations. Whether Mesmer helps her out or not. Is able to help.

She's well aware that he deals with neuropaths. All types and sub-types of neuropaths. She needs to sift these out.

The best are those individuals who've already had years of unsuccessful therapy.

Such as the old man from Vienna. Whose obstinacy in remaining in the courtyard was matched by the pains in his leg and the rash beneath his beard. All the things that made his life hell. Which he bellowed persuasively around the courtyard that morning. At an hour when, until recently, Anna would have still been asleep.

But recently that was over. Now Anna was long since awake. And to prevent her life from being made hell that day, she went out to see the bearded man.

He couldn't get down, the old man said. Gave her an

account of his suffering from the coach box. Mesmer's baffled by how she managed to get the heavily limping man into the house after all.

Through the man's beard the rash shone bluish-red. To treat his skin the beard had to go, Mesmer said.

The old man refused. He was a Jew. And had already suffered corporal punishment when he'd shaved once before. After a second time he'd have to leave the country.

Mesmer placed one hand on his back. The other on his hip. Could he feel any warmth?

Definitely. A fire. The old man began yelling. Bent over with spasms for ten minutes. Fell asleep. Anna stayed with him while Mesmer slipped into his laboratory. He couldn't keep the old man here. The house was full. He filled a bottle with water. Added some iron filings and nails. Stopped and secured the bottle with four nails in a wooden box. Called it a *magnetic box*.

When the old man woke up he could take it with him. To put beside his bed. No, better in his bed.

Later on he saw the old man walking to his coach, clutching the box. He stopped on the footboard. Lifted the box up onto the coach. Climbed behind it.

Word got around about this, too. And wove itself like a small, glittering thread into the magnificent stories people were now telling about Mesmer.

More people made the journey to see him. Anna sent most of them away.

To other doctors. In Vienna there were at least as many doctors as musicians. Störck and his consorts.

People were horrified when Anna said no. Then she would joke with them. As she had lately joked with the dog. And with the chickens when she crossed the courtyard to the stables. To let the coachman know. Frau Doctor wanted to go into town. To the tailor. To Vienna. To Störck. Or visit her friend. In Augartenstraße.

And recently she'd brought back something for everybody. For Maria a *hina ningyo*, a small Japanese puppet in bright-red silk. The *hina* would protect Maria wherever she was. Chocolate for Kaline. An amulet for the count. A mussel for the cook. Gloves for the coachman. A bone for the dog. And lots of buttons. Mother-of-pearl with yellow stones at the centre. From the button maker's on Kohlmarkt. Periodicals too, of course. Quills. Drawing paper. A pencil and the latest invention: an India rubber for Mesmer. Now he can "rub out" whatever he writes and draws. From the paper. Unlike his life. From which he can rub out nothing. Even if he should very much like to rub out what is about to happen.

He doesn't like the fact that, since the party, Anna has yet to come out of her good mood. Her efficiency mixed with frenzy. The way she stands in the kitchen. Laughing again already. Making coffee, which she's never done before. Bringing the hot pot to the table. Inviting Kaline over, pouring her a cup and one for the count and one for the coachman. Serving the servants. With a fresh cake. A burgher's wife bakes a cake. There's nothing wrong with this. Except for the fact that it's new. New and apparently unstoppable. New, like the look he has. He, who's turning into a tracking dog. Rooting out Anna as she wipes flakes of tobacco from the table. Flakes the count missed when he was shaking the contents of his scratched tin into the expensive one Anna gave him. And this new pleasure in his face. And Kaline, who is twirling between thumb and forefinger the fringes of a fine cloth Mesmer recognizes. Because it used to belong to Anna. Recently it has been sitting on Kaline's shoulders like a satire on what she usually wears. His searching eye drifts to the coachman; a far too expensive meerschaum pipe juts out from the corner of this man's mouth. The coachman greets him and averts his gaze.

Before Anna can say a word, Mesmer mutters that she must be mad.

Mad? she says, grinning. Or just generous.

Did she know the difference between generous and profligate?

Don't start that again, she says, turning away. Today everybody should get some.

Some what? he wants to know. What should everybody have some of?

Our success, she says.

Our? he says.

As things are going at the moment they're going very well, she says. We'll make it together. Didn't he think so? Why couldn't he just be happy?

She slides over a copy of the *Berlinische priviligierte Zeitung*.

Just in case he ever doubted himself or his work again.

The Letter from Vienna column has printed a missive from Court Secretary Paradis. It's bursting with joy at the unexpected, unexpectedly rapid curing of his supposedly incurable daughter. It would just be hurting himself to try to resist this wave of jubilation. Mesmer lets himself get carried along with it all.

Herr von Störck reads Prussian papers as well. And the empress. Not to mention von Kaunitz.

Congratulations, Anna says. He's done it. Now Berlin knows all about him and his method. That's an international breakthrough. He'd have patients in Prussia from now on.

She's as profligate with her praise as she is with her money, he says. What good is Prussia to him? He's from Lake Constance, an Aleman. And living in Vienna. What would he do in Berlin? International meant Paris, not Berlin. And it was really unfortunate that the letter wasn't in the *Wiener Allgemeine*. Ideally he'd have copied out the letter. Sent it to all his opponents. How often he'd have had to copy it out!

But it's unnecessary. There are newspapers in most Viennese coffee houses. And there's nothing in the world that the Viennese can't cut down to size with their chitter-chatter. And utterly. It's sickening how dependent he is on words. Even more so on printed ones. Anna poured some coffee. Put plate after plate in front of him. Laden with game and poultry pies, cheese, dried fruit and potato cakes. Preserved apricots and cranberries. Strudel. Vanilla milk. Pickled vegetables. And a basket of fresh rolls. All the things he loves. Unfortunately he often misses out on such pleasures. As he does today. Really misses out. No sooner has he swallowed the first mouthful than the doorbell rings. In a single gesture he restrains Anna and lets Kaline go. The expensive cloth flutters past him to the door.

A group, she announces. Several gentlemen and their wives. Wanting to congratulate the doctor. See the miracle girl.

Show them in. Anna is beaming uncannily.

She lifts her coffee cup as if it were a glass of red wine. His unstoppable wife. He is just able to fetch Kaline back with a whistle. Before Anna invites the whole rabble to join them at the table.

The visitors will have to wait. Where the patients wait. In the visitors' room. Or come back another time.

The young lady is sitting beside her Japanese doll, striking notes at the piano. She stops and travels up and down the keyboard with her fingers. As she once began. Years ago. She's blindfolded her eyes in the hope it will have a positive effect on her hands.

Apart from the mistakes she's got the lightest, most sensitive touch he's heard since Mozart, he says. Nonetheless he has to interrupt her. Her, the great hope. Not only for him. A light. Would she allow people to see her? Would she show herself? People are demanding to see her.

He expected her to say no.

People who can't play hate an audience. He'd magicked her eyes better and now her hands were sick. Let others try to understand that. She couldn't understand it. If anything she understood dogs' paws better than her own hands, she says. The great hope was beyond all hope. A light that had gone out.

Which Mesmer, with a few magnetic strokes, will fire up again.

They appeared before the people together. Shook hands. Told stories. Because everybody hopes for a story from the mouth of hope. And as stories never end in real life, the visitors started to develop the stories further. And some of them make Maria's story their own.

They covered her. Buried her. Under piles of words, phrases, questions, fragments of ideas, rattling, stuttering. Building sentences and dismantling sentences.

Everything just sticks to them. Boxing them in.

Even more people wanting to see her. The renowned doctor. And his miracle girl. If people cannot come in person they send servants. With greetings, wishes and presents.

It is only from the empress that nothing is heard. No word. No wishes. No presents.

It is just like the theatre. They appear, people applaud. They bow, people applaud. As if they were a troupe of actors or travelling artists. The dog, the doctor, the girl. Three colours. The black of the dog, the purple of the doctor, the girl in white. With a modest headdress while her hair is not long enough. And the people clap enthusiastically, egging each other on. Not just the dog. All three of them. There are always three of them.Maria wants it to be like that. And so shall she have it.

People bring bread, cakes, fruit. And drinks. Like at the opera. Maria plays piano for them. Simple pieces for simple people. For the easily impressible, mistake-forgiving people. The mistakes are becoming less frequent. He's not mistaken. And one thing's for certain: when she sings she makes no mistakes at all.

I was a poor little worm. She plays with the success of old. From her mouth it sounds irresistible. Wistful. Truthful. He's advised her to sing other songs. She thinks this one goes down best. With the people. And if you go down well with other people, you go down well with yourself, too. Applause was comfort for the loss of her hands.

Temporary loss, he corrects her.

Yes, she replies instantly. Temporary loss.

She is as swift as a highly reactive chemical. But easy to steer. How quick she is to accept things from him. Without any resistance. He's proud of this, too. How she benefits from him. That is his success.

It's important to survive the current moment, she continues. If you survive the moment you continue to live. That's why, at the moment, she can't do without the people and their applause. And she even enjoys their clapping. But less so the questions they pester her with.

Not just her. Him too. Even the dog. While Mesmer is quizzed on matters medical and Maria on her personal experience, they want to know everything imaginable from the dog. What the weather's going to be like. Or the coming harvest. They wake it up just as it's fallen asleep from exhaustion

Is that a dog? one man wants to know. Or a young lad under a spell?

While Mesmer and the girl perform what there is to perform with the Spanish cane, he entices it over. Prods it with his finger. Until the good-natured dog raises its head, wagging its tail. As far as the man posing the question is concerned, that is a resounding yes. But what does that mean now?

When the three of them appear before the public it's as if they were creating a wind. A friendly breeze puffing questions into people's minds. And these questions then suddenly pop up like ships from afar. And need somewhere to go. To a safe answer harbour. Mesmer's answers are not solid enough.

Herr Doctor, you've performed a miracle. How did you do it?

No, he hadn't performed a miracle. He was a scientist. And has developed a method.

What sort of method?

He'd discovered the most delicate substance in the world. He'd discovered the force, the *vis*, to guide it with.

A force, what sort of force?

Animal magnetism.

A magic force?

A natural force.

Did everyone have it?

More or less, yes.

More or less?

Yes, more or less.

So then anybody could have done it.

More or less, yes . . .

Including me? the man asking the question wants to know, starting to smile.

No, of course not.

Well what does that mean?

His explanations require explanations. Which branch out continually. Into the unknown. They take him to the point where even he's amazed at what he's achieved. With his hands.

And what his hands can do must be possible for other people's hands, too. Or so he assumes.

But still. No one else cured the girl. Not Störck, not Barth, no, none of these self-opinionated court toadies. Mesmer's explanations bewilder people, however. They will not understand him.

Then the expectant gazes cluster in the direction of Maria. The living proof must be able to explain what happened to her. But no, the living proof doesn't know anything either. About herself. And what happened. Maria feels full of holes. She has her answers ready for the questions which come time and time again.

Young lady, what's it like to be blind?

Like the colour black.

Young lady, what's the first thing you'd like to see when you leave here?

Schönbrunn. The Belvedere Palace. The imperial zoo. The turtles she knows from stroking them. And the savage apes. Which scream so loudly. She wonders whether they look as nasty as they sound. Or whether they disguise themselves with a smile.

Young lady, what's it like to be able to see suddenly?

Seeing is understanding, she says.

Understanding what?

Understanding distance, closeness. And understanding closeness from a distance.

Young lady, do you like being able to see?

Oh yes, she says. I love seeing. Seeing, she says, is like smelling. The hands are empty but what you see you have.

Does that mean that if you can see you don't feel so lonely?

No, she says. If you can hear, you don't feel lonely either.

But surely blind people are less engaged with the world?

171

No, she says. If a person with all five senses goes with a blind person to a social gathering, the latter is far more engaged. After all, they have to distinguish between all the voices, while the sighted person can survey everything. With a single look.

Young lady, what does your father think about your being able to see again?

He's delighted.

The people laugh, applaud. Maria curtseys. And again.

Then another question. She gets asked it every time. Maria calls it the pathetic one.

Young lady, are you not ashamed, as a young woman. Parading yourself in public like this?

No. For the thousandth time: No. She's not ashamed. She's a pianist. She doesn't parade herself. Quite the opposite. The world parades itself to her. And she, in return, allows this world to share. In her experience. But no more.

But, young lady, you are a young lady, are you not?

Yes, and? She's got no more to say on the subject.

She stands. For the thousandth time she stands. Shows her gratitude for the applause for the thousandth time. And then says for the first time: She feels like an ape. Her smile was a mask. A lie. She didn't want to be an ape.

She makes her way through the audience, disappearing up the stairs. Dragging a train of alarmed looks behind her. For the sighted as well as the non-sighted, the sick and the healthy, the hope of their life vanishes into thin air.

Is the young lady really well? one man dares ask.

She is. Definitely. Mesmer reassures him. Says her nerves

are a little frayed. That's all. A little worn by all the excitement. And because she can sense this, because she has an instinct, she has escaped.

The young lady's smart. Smart as a swallow, he thinks. That knows when it's time to come up from the lake in spring. Musicians are like swallows. Guided by an internal clock.

It's only him. He lets himself stay. He holds himself back.

Stays. Even though he can sense which way the wind is blowing. There's no longer a friendly breeze in the room. It's getting cold, stiff, spiky.

He looks at the iron spikes of the garden fence by the window. People are entering through the open gate. He watches them go in and out of his house. Watches them bringing in dirt. And he, he stays.

29 April, 1777

He stays. For Anna's sake. Who comes back from a visit to the dressmaker (the third this week) completely unnerved. He's never seen her like this. Dashing Anna, defiant of everything. And all of a sudden her gaze can no longer sustain his. Avoiding any closeness like a deranged animal.

After trying on clothes she had popped in to see her friend in Augartenstraße. The friend who usually congratulated her on her husband, and who envied her.

This time, however, Anna was told she might be fortunate in her choice of clothes. But in her choice of husband . . . ? Did she know what people were saying? No? Well, that her younger husband by a number of years was having an affair. Did she know that? No? Well. He'd made a young girl his slave. A blind girl. Using magnetism. His demonic power. His animal magnetism. Which, mind you, he was never able to explain to any God-fearing person under the sun. He was carrying on with the blind girl just as he fancied. Hadn't she noticed anything? Under her own roof?

Anna, worried about her own reputation, decides not to believe it, doesn't believe it. Not even now. This she swears.

Laughs as she says it, as if it were a funny joke. Then, abruptly, she starts shouting.

She'd set off and from all quarters people were offering her their sympathies.

The fact that she was letting him put his hands on her shoulders at this very moment shows just how needy she feels.

But still. He manages to calm her. He does not manage this with other people.

2 May, 1777

In the morning he climbs the steps to find a stranger beside the woodpile. An elegant cloth coat. A neatly tight plait. From which individual grains of powder float, like snowflakes in ice-cold weather. Pungent aromas. Standing there as if waiting for someone. As if he'd arranged a meeting at this very place. Kaline has let them down again. Left the door open.

What did he want?

Out there, the stranger says, his old mother was sitting in the carriage. She desperately needed Mesmer's help. He wanted to see whether the house was up to his mother's standards. So he was having a little look around. He's already gone past Mesmer. In the direction of the treatment room. Prods everything that gets in his way. Opens every door.

He's showing Mesmer around as if it were his own house. He strokes the backs of the armchairs and sofas in the drawing room. As if he were the magnetiser demonstrating his powers of animal magnetism. Only he touches everything and nothing is charged. Mesmer checks with his hands. The mirror, the glass in the mirror, the golden frame. The stranger briefly caresses the black cheeks of the bust of Mesmer and gives them a cursory slap. A bit of fun to build up trust. He laughs. Then continues along the mantelpiece.

The candle, the nautilus shell. Over to the red curtain. Which he draws to one side. He is already holding the Spanish cane.

Aha. He lifts it above his head. Pauses. Lunges out. A startled Mesmer recoils. The stranger makes a swishing sound as he swipes through the air with the cane.

So this is the magic wand. And where's the girl? The bewitched girl.

Instead of the old mother he'd said was in the carriage it's now the man's ill-mannered notions in the room. And he's not only thrusting a small crucifix at Mesmer. But calling him morally bankrupt, too. Seducing a defenceless blind girl.

Defenceless? That's how he feels when he asks the stranger to leave the house. Getting nothing but impertinent glares in return. Mesmer looks to the dog for help. Its tail wafts gently in the air while it waits anxiously to see who will dare do what next.

Mesmer says that as the dog is too polite to chase the man out, he'll have to do it himself.

He fails to notice that Anna is standing by the door until the stranger turns to her.

How could she put up with it? Where was her sympathy with the poor creature?

No doubt he can be heard throughout the house. But then only Anna. Anna's what remains of him. She has no trouble in shouting over the man. But her gaze remains fixed on Mesmer.

Is he a man?

You bet. She doesn't give him any other option. Just as he

used to have to drive the sheep from the meadow, standing very straight, his arms outstretched, like the scarecrows in the fields. This is how he drives the stranger to the door. For the first time in his life he single-handedly expels a man from the house.

He hadn't imagined it to be that simple.

Although he's toddling backwards the stranger is easily steered. The dog barks as if it were necessary to keep time. Not totally clear who he is barking at.

The stranger feels threatened. Clearly he hasn't a clue about dogs. The dog's barking at him, Mesmer, his master.

He'll write this up. With a note: Maybe the dog takes after its mother rather than its intelligent father. And mightn't that be a bit of proof for the legitimacy of ovulist theory?

He'll record it. As he will everything that attracts his attention over these days when the house is on its head. Or is it just the residents? And the strangers who are ruining the mood. Whereas his peers don't show their faces any more. The scientific community of Vienna deliberately look straight through him.

Vienna's provincial. He needs to think of his work. The small minds here will thwart it. They'll tear it to bits before it can be properly developed. He needs to get away. And he knows where. At night he lies beside the sleeping Anna, thinking of Paris where doctors are not just doctors, but *médecins–philosophes*. Who know that the human body is a machine. The finest machine in the world! And that there's a force that sets this machine in motion.

4 May, 1777

He's about to go into the garden nice and early, before the first visitors arrive, when he sees a heap of shit by the door. He almost stepped in it. He calls Kaline. He hadn't expected her to actually appear. But she's standing there. As white as a ghost. Or is that because of the garish colour of the cloth around her shoulders?

She is to get rid of the mess.

Her look of disgust when he dollops two small samples with a silver spoon onto the white of a porcelain bowl – what an impertinence, he thinks. But then, quick as a flash, she turns around. Throws up over the balustrade onto the spring flowers. Her mouth hidden behind the cloth, she stands up straight. Muttering her apologies.

Should he be worried?

No.

What had she eaten?

Same as the others. Tons of pancakes yesterday evening. It must have been the mess.

Then she should fast today.

Under the microscope he finds fibres and grains. Hard to identify the intestines it's passed through. Human or animal. Smells like animal. But the size and location militate against this. The fairly large heap was bang in the middle of the threshold. As if it had been deliberately left in the centre. He makes a note of his threshold discovery.

And: Strange how it fitted in with the Baroque facade. Animals possess all talents imaginable as well as a deeper sense. They often seem smarter than humans. Something proven by the periodic migrations of fish and birds, or by the way in which they sense danger and avoid it. But do animals have an aesthetic sense?

A question he would have loved to discuss with his friend Messerschmidt. In the Kramer coffee house. Beneath its vaults it's as dark during the day as it is at night. What he would give to be sitting there now. Opposite Messerschmidt. A candle between them. And two glasses of punch. A game of billiards afterwards.

But Messerschmidt is not in Vienna. Messerschmidt has been driven from Vienna.

6 May, 1777

Something makes him reassess his threshold discovery. Again at such an unGodly hour. The same place. Mesmer, with the same garden aim, puts the same foot on the same threshold. A resounding crunch. He withdraws his foot at once.

A bird. A raven, right across the threshold. Parallel to the house. He'll make a note of this. Same place. Where, like a shadow, a stain still marks the first discovery.

No trace of harmony this time. A raven is not a symmetrical affair. Across the middle. A raven is above and below. And head and tail always remain above and below. Even though in death they're flipped to the left and right. Threshold discovery number two disturbs him more than threshold discovery number one. Although the dead raven is undamaged on the outside, it suggests human violence. No animal would have left its prey just lying there like that.

The raven is still warm. Could it have died beneath his foot? Broken neck? The hypothetical broken neck swings in the air. Mesmer hoists the raven into the air. The dog snaps at thin air. The raven seems so lifelike. As if it were still flying, the blood beneath its shiny feathers. And Mesmer can hear sizzling in the rumour kitchens of Vienna. And he knows that it's him being fried.

In Paris people are tolerant, he thinks. Alert and interesting and tolerant.

7 May, 1777

He stays. For the sake of his patients. For the sake of their relatives. Who keep on surprising him. Like Herr and Frau Paradis. Who cannot make up their mind. The parents are humming and hawing. He's never known them like this. To begin with they just wanted to say hello to Maria. Then take her on a walk along the Danube. Then stroll from Kärntner Straße to Graben. It might get late.

Nothing against that. Maria's not his daughter. She's his patient. The ideal patient. In her new high shoes she scuttles to the coach like the empress's Lipizzaner horses. And is pressed in. Elegantly packed and tied up. With her travel wig. Topped by a bonnet.

He dissects the raven according to all the rules of the craft. As he once dissected corpses. He examines the nerve pathways. A bloody, stinking heap is piling up on a plate. He puts the plate by the window. The cat, wherever it may be when the window is opened, is there. Like Mesmer. Always there when hearts open up, when it's raining tears inside the house. As it does that evening. Through the chink in the door he can see the two girls sitting on the sofa. Maria's head on Kaline's chest. Kaline is stroking Maria's fuzzy mane which has grown substantially. The dog at their feet, the dog listening to the sobbing, which now points its ears in the direction of the door and wags its tail gently. The traitor. The traitor goes unnoticed. The girls are totally occupied with each other. And talking. About him.

According to Kaline he's strange. Late yesterday evening, when everybody was asleep, she saw him through the window standing outside. His arms were stretched up to the heavens. As if he were awaiting the answer from there.

What answer? Did he ask a question?

Kaline shrugs.

Maybe it was a prayer.

In the church she goes to, Kaline says, they put their hands together to pray.

So? Maria says. You can wait for an answer just like that, without any question. How long did he stand there?

She didn't know. She was just going to the chamber pot. On the way back he was still standing there.

But it's him the world is asking for, about everything.

Yes, Kaline says, she . . . also might have . . . to ask him.

Maria stops sobbing.

It's not so bad. Kaline is shaken by giggles accompanied by tears. Such horrible indigestion. Persistent. Nerve-racking.

The doctor can cure the simplest things with his Fluid, too. With his music and the leeches, Maria says. But helping her is not so easy. She's fighting back tears.

Her parents have taken her to see Dr Barth again. He led her past a large series of objects. Two of them she didn't recognize at all. She didn't know the words for them. She wasn't allowed to touch anything. She got three of the names wrong. She said rail for royal. Catch for coach. Books for box. And then they made her play that disastrous piece. The Haydn torture. Afterwards nobody spoke about Haydn. Only about her blunders. Dr Barth said she couldn't see at all. She was blind. And Mesmer's triumph a trick, a set-up. She gasps for air. A furious Störck immediately cancelled the appointment with the empress. There's more at stake than just the family's reputation. Of course. Tears aren't going to help. She needs to go home now. As soon as possible. She doesn't want to go home. She wants to stay with the doctor. Exercise her eyes and hands. An incomplete cure is no cure at all.

Another of his phrases she has adopted. But his pleasure at hearing this cannot offset the anger brewing inside him. It's so strong that his temples are starting to pound. He ought to have gone away long ago. But he stays. For Maria's sake.

⭐ CHAPTER THIRTEEN ⭐

12 May, 1777

The time has come. Maria's mother is at the door. Behind her, a tall, powerful servant. She looks small. Thin, vulnerable. A false impression. Mesmer has to invite the two of them in, as Kaline fails to do so. He invites them into the drawing room. He finds Kaline where she belongs. In the kitchen. Bent over a bucket.

She can peel the potatoes later, he says and then sees her vomiting into the bucket.

Stomach still troubling you?

Not as bad, she says.

How long's it been going on now?

No idea. Since the pancakes. A few days.

She's to bring tea and something sweet to the guests.

Let his wife, Riedinger and the count know, and then go to bed.

He'll look in on her.

*

He's not fazed when the mother says she's come to fetch her daughter. He knew it.

Of course. If she wished to bear the responsibility.

What responsibility?

For interrupting a cure, he replies. Shortly before its completion.

The doctor, she says, always uses so many words. My husband and I both consider this unnecessary.

Mesmer adds that if she takes her daughter back with her, she won't be able to count on his help in the event of a relapse.

That's regrettable, she says, but is not fazed either.

Only Maria. She throws herself on the ground. And as if her first and last days there had come full circle, all the old symptoms return. The spasms, the twitches, the rolling eyes.

Mesmer is beside her, placing a hand on her stomach as he always does. A mistake, perhaps.

The mother summons her daughter over. She stands up, clasped to Mesmer. For the mother this is merely the proof that all those wicked rumours are true.

Maria's in league with this man here, the mother screams, grabbing her daughter by the hair. She yanks her head back. The girl staggers. The mother pushes her daughter away. Slamming her into the wall.

The crashing attracts Riedinger as well as the powerful servant who, rolling up his sleeves, takes up position behind the mother again. While Mesmer carries the unconscious girl past the lot of them. Away from the warzone. Into the realm of mattresses. Where he ties magnets to her feet, stomach and chest. Covers her eyes with silk and begins the magnetic strokes.

He refuses to be disturbed. Not even when the door is wrenched open several times and closed again.

He only looks up when Court Secretary Paradis'ss dress sword narrowly misses him. A second thrust is parried by Riedinger. The court secretary's voice is trembling as he's shoved into the corner. Mesmer's knees are trembling. The girl isn't trembling. She is lying there as if dead.

If she were to lose her imperial honorary pension it would be Mesmer's fault alone. And he'd have to compensate for the loss. He's put the girl into a state of bewilderment. When she came here she was blind and could play the piano. Now she's blind and can't play any more.

Amidst all this there's one thing that sticks with Mesmer: a feeling of guiltlessness. There's no reason to feel guilty. Just as there's no reason for him to remain here.

One more thing before he goes, if the father takes the girl away from the house in this state, Mesmer can't guarantee anything. Even whether the girl will survive.

ⵣ CHAPTER FOURTEEN ⵣ

21 May, 1777

The cooing begins at dawn. The family of pigeons starts the day with some gentle, early proceedings. Soft bird voices conferring with one another, a touch monotonous, these can get cross in a trice at the slightest disturbance. Like the old bags in St Stephen's Cathedral. Incessantly muttering their prayers. Never-ending lamentations about the state of the world. This plot of depravity and corruption. Where nobody knows who they can still trust.

She thinks of Riedinger, who called her parents' offensive an unsuccessful attempt to steal her away. And how she jumped down his throat. Unsuccessful? What was unsuccessful about it? Her health had been brutally stolen from her. And she'd got this terrible nervous fever. Semi-conscious for almost a week. Only a daily ration of magnetic treatment got her back on her feet again.

But, he'd replied softly, the main thing was that she was together here with him, and that they could continue to play Mozart together.

She's allowed to stay. Until she's back in full working order. Full working order. The sound of it. It's her father's phrase. Who thinks she can be repaired like a faulty clock. And when she's seeing and ticking again and pointing to things and knows what they're called, and playing the piano without mistakes, then he'll take her home. His little pianist. Back to the Rüssel. To her two pianos. Whose sound she can recall as if it lived in her ears. But she lacks any knowledge of what it sounds like when she talks to her parents.

Her father hasn't a clue of what actually happens to her here. How could he? She can't explain it. And there's nothing wrong with her father. The doctor never touched him. On the contrary. The doctor banished him from the house. With his powerful voice. And her father, who usually doesn't take orders from anybody, is sticking by it.

And what, pray, to threaten Kaline with if she doesn't come to wake her soon? If she just leaves Maria to the pigeons? Nothing. You can't threaten someone who isn't there. You have to do without her, as well as the hot, foaming chocolate she would have brought.

Maria gets dressed on her own, goes down the stairs and sits in the leather armchair. Waits like a ghost by the cold fireplace. Kaline says that the dog barks ghosts away. But the dog approaches her with a yawn. Has a thorough stretch. Lays its muzzle on her shoe so she can't slip away unnoticed. While he sleeps and twitches, panting slightly, as he dreams he's being chased by ghosts. He's frightened of them. How frightened Kaline is of ghosts. Even though she's been behaving like one herself recently. Dissolving into thin air. Vanishing. Into the depths of the house. Scattering everything to the wind, herself and her duties, chores and friendships.

And how, pray, is Maria to explain Kaline's disappearance? The search for Kaline is the search for an explanation. And will find Kaline strangled by her silk scarf. And also shot, stabbed, poisoned. Quartered. Innocent, left lying there in blood. That's too much even for Maria. She wiggles her toes and the dog leaps up instantly.

Stupid mutt, she snarls at it, horrified. And the dog, squarely on all fours, shakes itself. Indignant, baffled at her extraordinary lack of consideration. Even though it's merely an expression of her helplessness.

She finds Kaline in the evening. After all. And by chance. And totally intact. If a little inert. Maria touches her slightly hunched body. In the room off the washing room. On a pile of unwashed bed linen.

What's wrong? What's she doing holed up in here? Had she eaten?

No.

Why was she putting her stomach through it? First stuffing herself, then fasting.

No reaction.

Was she freezing?

No. Kaline sounds weak. But responsive.

That's good. Maria has lots to tell her. About her session with the doctor. His hands. And how the places he touches get hotter and hotter. Until they're glowing. And soft, warm balls are rolling through her veins. In all directions. Into her arms, legs, fingers, toes. And back again. It's hard to believe that it's your own body, the softness, the warmth, the burning sometimes, highly animated. She'll tell the doctor. He'll treat Kaline. Then Kaline will know what she's talking about.

But the best thing, she says, this was the best thing: She felt like a note from Riedinger's violin. Resonating brightly and clearly throughout the rooms, and beyond, out through the windows. A note from Mozart she's playing together with Riedinger. The sonata for piano and violin. You know the one?

Is Kaline trying to shake or nod her head? Hard to tell. Her neck seems too weak for either.

The frightfully beautiful second movement. That Mozart sound with the semitones. That sound whose song is like the world. And which leaves you in bits.

More mysterious than anything she's ever heard. More mysterious than the most mysterious mystery. And the doctor wanted to know again what she was thinking. Although he probably thought he knew anyway. And just wanted to check that his suspicions were correct. It was important. Clear. The doctor and the things he found important.

She'd been thinking of Mozart, she said. He said he'd been thinking of Mozart, too. Should I have believed him? She'd been thinking of a sonata.

And he said, G major. The *allegro spirituoso*.

Exactly. And then the doctor started humming the tune. The very one.

Strange, she said, that the same music was playing at the same time in the same place, in their heads.

192

The doctor's not surprised at all. He hadn't expected anything different. But she didn't find that particularly *spirituoso*. After all, she could have been thinking of Bach or Haydn.

Yes, the doctor said. But the important thing was that she'd been thinking of Mozart because he was thinking of Mozart.

And before she could say that the reason why she'd been thinking of Mozart was that she couldn't get his music out of her head. That she'd wanted to meet him for ages. To play for him . . .

He said: I've invited him. The little, great Mozart.

Kaline, she says, what does one say to that? He's invited him. Zartmo.

Two syllables which bear no fruit with Kaline. She's lying there. As if abandoned by everything. Including herself. While Maria's positively thriving when she thinks of the words: seeing Mozart. Seeing him make music. Making music, making music.

That's what the doctor promised. As long as she, the young lady, wasn't opposed to it.

The very opposite of opposed. She'd just been thinking what she might play for him. A good question, a really good question.

Playing Mozart to Mozart was not a good idea. No. After much dithering she decided on something of her own. The *sicilienne*. Her best piece.

So after the session and obligatory resting time, she, Maria, had gone straight back to the piano room. Where Riedinger, her dear friend, her right hand, her very first ear, once again demonstrated his friendship towards her. And skipped his lunch to play music with her. Where would she be without Riedinger?

Without his hearing. His hearing is so precise. He hears every mood, every note. And understands them. And every atmosphere. In every rest.

You can't take this for granted. Most people can't hear anything, even if they try. They fail to hear, as Dr Mesmer might express it if this activity were given an expression. But this man, Riedinger, was always engaged with his hearing, as was his entire body. And his fingers. Or hand or foot. She needed only to nod and he would make a note of what he'd just heard. And say something about it.

Whether it was a *sicilienne* or a horse charging away in six–eight time.

Mozart was coming, she said. Was he aware of that?

And? With a shrug of his shoulders Riedinger showed that he was the second person unfazed by the mention of Mozart.

He'd been here before. Plenty of times.

And is he nice?

Naturally, it did not escape Riedinger's attention that her question was inappropriate.

But once again he stood the test. As her friend and supporter. Didn't give anything away. Merely said that it wasn't the sort of attribute he'd ever thought of judging Herr Mozart by.

Just like that, very coolly.

As you wish, she said.

Well, he added, perhaps you could call him a bit special, Herr Mozart.

What did that mean?

She'd see. At least she would if she'd consider removing her blindfold.

Is Kaline still listening to her? She's nodding in any case. Clearly. But it's a strain for her to lift her arm, to put it over her face.

Of course, who wouldn't take off their blindfold for Mozart.

She'd take everything off for Mozart, she'd said. And Riedinger had cleared his throat. In the way he always cleared his throat when she made a mistake at the keyboard and played a wrong note.

She wanted to encounter Mozart with as many senses as possible, she'd added quickly. Riedinger muttered that this sounded like nonsense to him, and then apologized instantly. His pupil was already waiting for him at the Naschmarkt. He had dashed out.

She wanted to hear Mozart. Smell him. See him. Most of all she'd love to feel him. Like the squeaky, twisted Messerschmidt heads in Messerschmidt's workshop. Where Mesmer had taken her. These artificially artificial heads. With the strangely distorted faces. Which she didn't know whether to laugh or scream at.

And all of a sudden he was there.

I liked Mozart from the word go. He was like something symmetrical. Well rounded. His voice alone. Bright and with a heart. A round one. Never spiky. And his hands. Hardly bigger than hers. Could such a small hand master the keyboard, she wondered? What nonsense, she thought. She managed it, didn't she? He'd read her *sicilienne*. And knew at once that she liked dancing. She, who could only hear but not read music, had been impressed by this. Even though it was obvious. With a *sicilienne*.

He'd merely hummed the melody and taken it a little further.

What luck that she was allowed to compose. He had a sister. She wasn't allowed to any more. Which made both of them sad. It wasn't that she couldn't. She'd learned composition and was very adept at it. Always able to find an interesting bass voice for any well-worn melody. Which she then developed elaborate variations on. As often as she wished. And that was enough variations for their father. Accompany, yes. Compose, no. She's going to get married after all. So their father was keeping her talent on a short leash.

Being too talented was not helpful. For a woman. Who wanted to find a man.

And this, it seemed to him, was the very first time in both their lives that their father had not been thinking about him first.

But he, he was allowed to do both. Able to do everything. And could feel this archetypal femininity within him. Indeed, without this feminine, dance-like aspect within him he wouldn't be capable of putting two notes together.

At that moment, Kaline, Maria says, she sensed something. Between him and her. Something yearning for a higher power to become harmony. The doctor would probably call it magnetism. Magnetism was an entire ocean of things in common.

He was hungry. As was she. When they took coffee he was always grabbing the same biscuits as her. The dark, moist ones. He didn't just like them. He was crazy for them. So crazy that her hand was always touching his in the biscuit basket. His hand, like hers, rummaged past the buttery pale biscuits dusted in icing sugar, to the bottom. And they instantly devoured what they hauled up.

And he said, now it's time for the pale ones to meet their maker.

After this it was only our fingers touching in the basket. Pianists' fingers called away from their playing, smeared brown and licked. Fingers which couldn't get enough of anything. Which is why, Maria says, she'd rung for Kaline. She, Kaline, had remained the greatest absence of the afternoon. Only the dog came trotting along. And the two of them had held out their hands. Which it had very much enjoyed licking clean. All four of them. And Mozart had assumed that there was nobody else in the house besides the three of them. And even though she'd not been able to say with absolute certainty whether this was true or not, she'd heard a tone of regret in his voice.

Maybe he'd have liked to play cards.

A game of tarock. But not with two! To offer him something, she'd offered to show him her natural history collection. Her multitude of snails and mussels. The medical worms.

He'd agreed at once. Regrettably.

They hadn't lingered long over the mussels, stones, leaves

197

and feathers. But they did when it came to the sleeping snail. Which he weighed up in his hand, comparing how heavy it was to the empty snail shells. Turned it over and around. Put it to his nose and sniffed. And tapped the sealed shell. Was the thing inside still alive? It fascinated him. Even though he couldn't say why. Instead he asked her why she was so fond of these slimy little beasts. And she'd said that she envied the snails. Because they could extend and retract their eyes. As they pleased. She'd love to be able to do that. Surely that was the ideal set-up. Having eyes that you could make disappear. And then the leeches. These interested him. Even though all he could see was green water. And so he rapped on the glass. As if to wake them.

Put his hand in? No, he didn't want to do that. He laughed but, joking *à part*, he found worms creepy.

He had moistened his finger and started rubbing the rim of the glass. Producing a note. A piercing D sharp. Like the doctor at his glass machine. And shortly afterwards another note: a loud, splitting crack. And it was wet around the glass. And all this only because Kaline had put too great a demand on her stomach and not responded to Maria's ringing.

Later, at the piano, Mozart had sat behind her. Where Riedinger usually sits. She'd launched straight into her *sicilienne*. Played it well. Delicately and buoyantly, and in spite of a few little slips she'd remained totally calm.

Unlike Mozart. Who'd wriggled about on his chair and then suddenly, in a flash, shot forward with it. Sat beside her, at the keyboard. And held his breath, which made her stop in fright.

Breathe on, breathe on, he said. And: Which keys do you prefer to play, Fräulein, the dark or light ones.

What?

No, which? Which did she prefer? The black or white ones? While she thought about it his hands pounced on the black ones. And then clambered up all the keys playfully. He played her *sicilienne* for her.

Had she ever tried it quicker?

No. Never.

Did she like it? It was at least possible.

Where he's right, he's right.

She didn't say any more. All of a sudden she understood the moment precisely. And let it pass.

But then he asked her about his keystroke. Whether she liked it. She said yes. Liked it a lot.

Yes? So what's it like?

Yes. Like rain perhaps. Like rain falling at an angle. Or pearls. Dropping into the grass.

They'd laughed.

Later she became serious. When he got up. And she thought he wanted to pop out of the house, over to the privy. But he had stroked her head and said she was a genius. And he wanted to compose something for her.

And then, before he left the room, he turned round and called out, *Ostentatio vulnerum*. Show your suffering. With these words he'd vanished into the house.

As she'd neither heard him come or go she wasn't sure if she'd dreamed the whole thing. And, dream or not, she had to admit that she'd hardly missed Kaline all day. It was only now that she was missing her. Because she was lying here bent double, not saying a thing.

Hello?

Nothing.

How was her stomach?

Nothing.

Maybe her hand could provide some comfort. She must have been eating pancakes again. What did the doctor say?

Kaline sits up.

The doctor said a child wasn't a pancake. And his wife said she'd pray for her. But the shame, she said, had to leave this house.

And for the birth the doctor recommended one of those houses where women like her were able to bring their children into the world. And after the birth he recommended not cutting the umbilical cord. Otherwise, he said, the child would get the pox later on. Something she surely didn't want. A child lacerated with scars.

⊷ CHAPTER FIFTEEN ⊶

Tünsdorf, June, 1777

Is it a journey or flight? Is it attracting him or driving him? He calls the force attracting him Paris. Even though Paris is a city rather than a force. And the other pole, which is actually a city but feels like a force at his back, and which is driving him away, he calls Vienna. The question as to which of the two forces has greater influence, the pulling or pushing, is what is weighing down on him most heavily.

He spent hours thinking about it in the stagecoach. And what are thought processes like in a stagecoach? As a general rule, movement and thought are mutually beneficial. As long as one's thoughts can resist the soothing, massaging plodding of four carthorses. Whenever he looked out of the window he expected to find a new distinct thought behind each hill they plodded past.

Paris. Paris, he's heard, is not like other cities the end of a journey, but the beginning. Which he was longing for as ardently as the end of this coach journey. He felt more exhausted than the horses when he saw how they hung their heads at the stations. They were exchanged. He was not.

Roughly in the middle between Vienna and Paris, perhaps a little closer to Paris, he had got out. Had stayed at a mill. In a room filled day and night by the whooshing of the millstream.

He can hear water from the narrow bed. And when he lifts his head he can see water. Plunging down a rocky precipice towards him as if it were trying to wash him away. The house along with the room, the table along with the chair, the bed along with him. But then it turns the bend after all and shoots towards the mill wheel. Which turns and turns.

He can feel the damp, cool air on his skin. He asked the miller for a second, then a third blanket. He had to shout, shout over the water. A maid brought him the blankets, the second, the third. Hammered on the door to his room so that his bed shook. The people here don't speak. They let the water do the talking. In its polyphonic whooshing. Penetrating the mill like a silence. Into which he introduced a sound. He'd opened the window, unpacked the glass armonica, set it up and started to play. What luck that there's just enough space for the armonica in his room. This tiny room, barely half the size of the magnetic baquet. Which he's left in Vienna. In Anna's care.

She'd said he was mad. To choose to travel by normal stagecoach. Had he lost his mind? Why wouldn't her husband go by calash at least? By calash for her sake.

She said nothing more about his Paris fantasy. Apart from the fact that she understood he wanted to get away. And that he'd be on his own in a calash. Able to think. Talk to himself as much as he liked. Save time. And being wedged in next to strangers . . . having strangers rubbing up against you, she said. Paris shouldn't stand between them like some great unknown. He should have a break from himself and from the Viennese and their habits, but not from her. Hence the sound advice to travel in a calash.

He didn't want to disagree with her, he disagreed, but people didn't bother him. She ought to know how much he enjoyed meeting people. They were always interesting somehow. And he was in full health. And strong enough. Still.

She knew that, Anna had said, adding, Go on then. He'd be the one responsible for the consequences.

He wanted to travel as everybody else did. Any other way was a waste. But he didn't say this. It was a trigger. Which would have made Anna explode at once. And he wanted an easy departure, an easy one which would make his return easy. So he'd told her, almost *en passant*, that he needed some time to himself. Needed a change. But didn't tell her that inside him was a powerful invalid competing with a weak man in full health. It was something he couldn't articulate, and Paris at least was something which fitted his symptoms.

Anna had flared up briefly. Raising her beautiful voice. Nobody could feel so threatened so suddenly as his Anna. He couldn't just leave her sitting here, she screamed.

But when he placed his hand on her arm and asked her to stand in for him, the doctor, because he knew what she was capable of in his absence, without the presence of his indescribable power, he felt she was placated.

She promised to throw herself into the breach. She

promised to hold the fort. She promised to look after the baquet. For as long as was necessary. After she had overcome her shock she had given him a night-long farewell which already gave him hope for a tender and intimate reunion.

And then early the next morning, wrapped in a new, black-and-beige-striped, fashionably shimmering provocation he'd never seen before, she'd accompanied him to the post station in Vienna, pointed to the ivory-coloured lace and whispered that it came from where he was going. Got out of the coach with him, whispering that the sooner he was gone the sooner he'd be back. And led him, her hand on his forearm as if they were about to dance, over to the black-and-yellow stagecoach, a good match for her dress she thought. Scornfully she eyed the stagecoach gleaming in the morning sun and called it a hornet stealing away her husband. Declared the horses rested and the *postillon* sober – a slice of good luck. She'd stood still, and when he made to kiss her goodbye, guided him past her shining lips, which gently breathed the words: *À bientôt*. No tears when he got in. She merely lowered her gaze when the coach set off. He waved goodbye. And suddenly discovered this new expression on her face. A hint of petrifaction. It made him think of an animal in winter. Hungry. Sitting there silently. Surrendering to the snow and human beings. Frozen. Withdrawn.

How many borders awaited him! How much fuss over passports, trunks and bags and customs! Every traveller knows this. He had learned his text for the border guards by heart. All the things that were in his trunks and why. Of course the border guards never hear what he says, but always infer the opposite. What he hasn't said. They're fixed on what isn't in his bags or his lists or his thoughts. They infer it. As if ghost words were slipping out of his mouth between real ones. Which only border guards can hear. Because when they hear them they feel a little less superfluous. A little more important. Just because of this one of them is always sure. Rubbing his hands as he eyes Mesmer's luggage. Rummages silently through the bags. But doesn't find it, the ghost, the thing that's been promised.

Door closed. And off goes the stagecoach. Another border behind him. The Viennese medical fraternity. The empress. And the snippets of news which zip around amongst the Viennese like the finches in high summer before the hunting season.

As early as Linz he started feeling the consequences Anna had alluded to. His bottom honed black and blue from sitting on the wooden bench. When he was a boy by the side of the road he had envied the well-to-do ladies. Imagining that their expansive dresses would protect them from such effects. Didn't well-to-do ladies always sit down as if in a lush, soft nest, no matter where they took a seat?

It was through his patients that he first discovered he was wrong in this. And Anna had taught him very graphically the level of sacrifice hiding beneath the opulence of this packaging.

One of these many-layered packages had got on in Karlsruhe. Squashed herself next to him on the thin leather cushioning. Endeavouring to keep the mass of material under control, she'd told him straight away: Normally she hired a carriage for herself alone. It was just that this time he, who else, had got there first. But she'd manage.

Her servant brought in her luggage. A huge birdcage covered with wine-red velvet, which he placed on the other bench, setting it opposite his mistress. He went away and came back three times, on each occasion piling up a vast amount of small strapped-up cases, small tied-up crates, and small laced-up boxes around the velvety cover. Revealing the secret he left the cabin without a goodbye.

Bluebeard, the woman announced, taking away the velvety cover. A mature specimen of the species *Amazona festiva*, probably older than the two of them put together. According to Linnaeus's *Systema natura*, he knew it was a macaw, no more and no less.

And he, she said, must be a man of learning.

A naturalist, he said. And doctor, he added.

She was Henriette, Madame Henriette.

She'd thought he might be a doctor. He clearly looked like one. A doctor on the road, she added, that was something quite particular. Particularly gratifying. With a doctor on board she immediately had the feeling she was in good hands. Cared for and protected.

He had to disagree with her. First, doctors were always on the road, it practically went with the job. And second, most of them went off track quite easily. And once off track a doctor gets more and more lost. Because doctors are only ever thinking of the road ahead, rather than focusing on their own path and reorienting themselves.

Interesting theory, she said. Where was he going to?

Paris, he said. Paris to begin with.

To begin with? Wasn't Paris enough?

He wanted to visit all the capital cities of Europe. To be more specific, it was the scholars of Europe's capital cities which attracted him.

Well, Henriette said. He had a lot ahead of him. Her late husband's hobby had been ornithology. So he might have been on his list, too. But he was dead now. And he hadn't written down his research findings, or disclosed them to her. Only to the parrot. He'd shared everything with it. But it didn't talk to her.

The bird was now trying to spread its wings.

Look, Henriette said. Its eyes. That look. As if it had been copied – from her dead husband. He'd got the creature from a Spaniard, a peacock as they say. She'd often thought of giving the animal some of her eyelashes . . . putting them below its blue crest . . . sticking them above its bare goggle eyes.

Also: Bluebeard was forever trying to escape. Look, the nicks in the bars. The bird hadn't said a word since its master died. And recently it had started plucking out its feathers. Did he know about parrots, too?

Mesmer watched the bird which now had its head at an angle and was hanging from one of the bars of the cage. There must have been more than three dozen of these bars, but this very one was preventing Mesmer from looking away.

When the horses started moving the bird dropped its wings apathetically. Only when the coach reached a bend did the blood-red of its down feathers quiver between the bars and flutter through the thin layer of sand on the bottom of the cage. There are sounds that Mesmer cannot bear. Feathers rubbing against wood or metal, for example feathers against bars. Feathers only sound good in the air.

And after every bend the bird would crap in the sparse sand on the floor of the cage. But without eating or drinking the whole time, a time which dragged on and on. Mesmer immediately set about trying to work out where on earth the bird was getting the stuff from that was dropping from it, or rather dripping. While its owner, dressed in velvet cut from the same roll as the nightcap of the bird – which was substantially larger than a cubit – tried to distract it with language exercises.

Emphasized *Bluebeard.*

Repeated *Bluebeard.*

Raised her index finger.

I. Am. Your. Little. Bluebeard . . . I. Love. You . . . I. Talk. To. You.

Nothing. A mute parrot with a bare patch on its chest. To cover up her embarrassment she stuck all sorts of goodies between the bars. Little apple wedges and pieces of bread. Salad leaves. Ears of millet. Biscotti. Dried apricots and plums. Hazelnuts. Until the cage looked as if it had been dressed into costume. Or like one of those Arcimboldo heads.

And the elegant bird suffered. This instantly transferred itself to Mesmer. He suggested taking the animal out. Provoking a hysterical reaction from the velvet woman, who called her animal a beast.

Mesmer undid the bolt. Opened the little door. Saw the frozen gaze which the bird was now fixing on his hand. And could already feel the plumage. And the bird recoiling at his attempt to grab it. He stroked the splayed wing feathers which changed in colour from yellow to sulphur.

Mesmer closed his eyes. All that remained of this magnificent foreigner was a Viennese raven. The magpies and jays at Lake Constance.

After a while he withdrew his hand, the bird was clinging to the bars upside down, and Henriette was still grumbling, albeit half-heartedly, about how he could dare touch her late husband's macaw, when the parrot interrupted her. Said right in the middle of her scolding, *Is Albert there with you? And if so, how? – God forgive me this question.*

In its squeaky parrot voice. And its right eye, this black mirror gaping from a nest of yellow down, met the embittered stare of its mistress. Who complained that her late husband had never read to her. Although he did to the bird. The bird. It had memorized everything. Now, surely, it had to share with her all that her husband had read to it. No doubt it could recite novels by heart. It couldn't be allowed to keep these to itself. The smart animal. The smart and wicked animal, she said. He could take her word for it.

But she could now see that, with his help, everything would turn out for the best. Proof of this was that the bird had just spoken. He was a true magician, she said, getting out with Mesmer. She'd stayed in the mill with him. Had barged into his room in the middle of the night, the cage in her hand.

Let him tell her how he'd done it. The bird was completely changed.

They spent the entire night together. The parrot gabbled away, which disturbed nobody as the millstream was so loud and Henriette was sitting close to Mesmer. He'd told her about his discovery. And she'd asked questions about the nature of his Fluid. Intelligent questions he'd have imagined beyond her. A matter. An ethereal matter he called it, emphasizing the word matter, so that the following morning she wouldn't think she'd spent half the night with a magician.

After so many days in the stagecoach he feels as if he's been beaten up. No wonder people believe in magic. Who wouldn't wish to fly from one place to another? Fly over borders. Especially fly over aches in the back and limbs. Painful bottoms and intrusive thoughts. Such as those about Linnaeus's theory on the sexuality of plants.

The detour he'd taken at Lake Constance would also have also been easier to suffer had he flown. He'd wanted to see his parents. The lake. The fresh reeds. And the meadows sloping down to the water, which at this time of year were shooting upwards. And beneath the trees the rebellious blossoming of the masses. And the lake, which never looks younger, never softer than in early summer. Compared with the millstream by his window, a dozing sun-reflecting giant. Becoming over-grown from all sides. Until the bank vanishes beneath the undergrowth. And nobody knows where the men with their axes in the knee-deep water have come from. Where they lie in wait for the fish that have been drawn to the bank to spawn. Rich pickings for the evening.

His mother's face when he surprised her in the kitchen. How her face brightened up. And then darkened again imme-diately. As if she couldn't be happy. But she can be happy. He knows this. Just as he knows that her happiness always gives rise to this note of reproach. As if happiness were an impertinence. Too much of a good thing.

Where had he been all this time? She'd expected him earlier. At Easter. They'd written about him in the paper, in the *Constanzisches Wochenblatt*. That's where things had got to. She was finding out about her son from the newspaper. Which she couldn't read. The priest had to be so kind. To read to her. What it said. About her son. And he's chosen today to come. Today of all days. When his father has left. To see the archbishop. And won't be back until next week.

What's more, she'd said, he looked worse than ever. She'd always known that Vienna was a nothing place. That world-wide Vienna. And that widow. An ancient woman. Almost as old as me, she said. And she was his mother. As if he could ever forget that. That's what comes of it. And although he had an inkling, he asked what she meant.

What comes of what?

No children, she said. You haven't been blessed with a child, have you?

In her dialect it sounded as if she were talking about a child being sawn in two. And it occurred to him that his old home was no longer how he imagined it in Vienna.

But he does have a son, he replied.

Not one, she said, who's related to her. She lit a fire, put the pan on the hearth. How long was he staying?

He was just passing through. He lied. He had to go on, to Strasbourg. An important patient.

His mother went silent. Like the whitefish and perch dusted

in flour on the wooden board beside the pan. At least the fish smelled as they used to. And tasted as they used to. What Danube fish could be a match for perch? The following day he resumed his journey. Took a boat to Konstanz and there climbed aboard the stagecoach. It was flight, pure and simple, which put him back on track. But the fact that he was fleeing in the direction of Karlsruhe was all down to the powerful attraction of Paris.

Before he'd left Vienna he'd leafed through Störck's writings. Read the bit about hemlock. Marvelled at how clearly and intelligently von Störck wrote. And made a mental note to write as clearly himself. To translate what actually happens in the magnetic sessions. Happens to him. Happens to the patients. What happens between them the moment his hands touch another person's skin and a barrier opens.

Describe the barriers. Describe the flow. The flowing. Describe the Fluid. Describe this innermost of all substances. Its qualities. Invisible, nameless, continual and extremely subtle.

And confront the missing words head on – make do with water words. Words written as if for the millstream. And. Describe the millstream. The surging and roaring. The rivulets, the little affluents which babble as they pulsate, flow, shimmer, throb, trickle, slow and then surge forth again.

He needs to draw up a scale. From roaring to barely perceptible. Develop an apparatus. A sort of electroscope. Specifically for the *Vis magnetica*. Which is finer than its electric sister. He needs to determine a size. A unit of measurement. Write down what happens when the patients fall into that sleep which he calls magnetic. When faces become wildly contorted. Or somebody starts shouting almost imperceptibly. Or when they talk, talk, talk. Desperate for him, who is describing them. Articulating his thoughts. Or hating him or themselves, the described. He needs to make a note of emotional tempests. The oceans of tears.

What he cannot measure he needs to write down. He needs to find a method for measuring. Construct an apparatus. Describe it at least. As if it were an electrostatic machine. Which any old fool can build these days. The magnetic force is strong. As strong as the electrical one. But it's finer. And never destructive. Which means it's more useful. The future will prove it. If he succeeds. In translating it. Into a language of the future.

All those things which Störck will never be able to write about. Because he can only write about measurements. Störck's hands. His chubby, pink doctor's hands. Nails cut short, well-cared-for fingertips, dextrous, attentive, industrious, tidy fingers. But deaf to the essence of things. This is why the baron has no idea what hands are capable of. He should, could, must write this down finally. No one beside him is able to do it. At all events he must extend the scope of his hands, which at the moment is limited. He must reach out to more people than those who he's reaching out to with his hands.

He can write, he can read. More and more people can write and read. They all want him to reveal something. Something about his method. But there's no secret there. He simply believes that he'll reach out to more people with words about his method than with his hands. It's not his method which is the entrance ticket to the academies, but the revealing of his method. But he must keep these thoughts secret. Still. He can't just hand them over. Send them away indiscriminately, without knowing in whose hands they might end up. The world is teeming with grabbing charlatans, quacks, wannabe doctors, pretend invalids, money-makers, bogus healers and thieves.

In any case, not every experience is suitable for committing to paper. His least of all. He can only do what he does. And the magnetic force does the rest. It does what it wants. It can't be captured. Maybe, like light, it can be increased with mirrors, it can also be reproduced and increased through sound. But otherwise it is an enigma. An enigma which is impossible to capture. A flowing enigma, for which there is no language. At least none that he can master. And after all, this is what the discipline known as science is all about. Mastering. And articulating. Taming. Drawing. Making clear. Making repeatable. And representing.

He'd just put Störck's text back on the shelf when there was a knock and the coachman passed him two letters through the crack in the door. Ever since Mesmer had ordered Kaline to rest and she was just lying on the bed in her room, the coachman was overdoing it in his attempt to be coachman and housemaid in one. From early in the morning to late in the evening he darted back and forth between the house and stables.

Mesmer beckoned him to come in. He looked so thin, he ought to take a break.

Outside, the coachman replied, a crowd of people were waiting, and in the cellar the washing needed to be folded.

Perhaps, Mesmer had said, it would be advisable to close the front gate.

The coachman avoided his gaze. Muttered that in all the years he'd been working here he couldn't recall the front gate ever having been closed.

The first letter, from Störck, in typical Störckesque handwriting, was a sharply worded demand.

Mesmer should release the girl right away. There must finally be an end to his skulduggery, otherwise the baron would take steps.

Mesmer had not imagined that the end could be standing there so abruptly at the door. Just as he couldn't imagine that the reasonable and usually friendly Störck, the industrious and meticulous authority on plants, could talk about him so harshly, so unfairly. After all the man had not only been a witness at his wedding, but had also witnessed Maria's progress. The letter was all the more painful because he held Störck in high regard. His zeal. And now he was behaving as if truth were a woman. Belonging to only one man: him, Störck. And the moment he noticed that Frau Truth was giving a friendly eye to another man, he held it against him. In truth, however, Frau Truth is not so precise with the truth.

The second letter, written less pedantically, sounded more conciliatory. A short, hurried note. The court secretary was thinking of spending a few days in the country with his family. And so wanted to come and fetch his daughter who was surely recovered by now. Didn't want to miss a minute of the country air. Which did everyone the world of good. Him, his wife, and the young lady. So he'd come tomorrow – same time. If it were so desired, he'd bring the girl back. What's more he was looking forward to seeing his daughter. And, whether he believed it or not, the doctor too. And he remained, etc. A scrawl.

Later on he read the letter to Maria. She listened silently. Without crying, which surprised him. She had listened and then said nothing. He hadn't said anything either and it was a while before she said she wanted to know what he intended to do this time.

This time, he'd said, there was nothing more to do.

She'd gone up the stairs to her room. More sluggishly than usual, which horrified him. Like an old woman, he thought, watching the dog push past her so it could greet her upstairs with a wagging tail.

And the many fears he harboured. That the changes ahead might manifest themselves in the form of a somatic disorder brought on by nerves. Such as paralysis of the limbs. Which her sluggish gait might just be the beginning of. He'd followed her. But had abandoned his suspicions when he saw how adroitly she folded her dress. And how deftly her hands gathered together the wig and all the accessories to the theatrical production that was her hair. The birds' nests, the eggs, the tiny bells, all the many different details. She packed them one on top of the other in her velvet-lined trunk. Her bright voice announced that she had thought of something new for the next wig which would inevitably come her way at the Rüssel. The bird theme was terribly passé now, like a well-sucked thumb. Her next hair production had to show something new: the magnetic force. She'd tie small magnets to her hair. Pearls of amber. Wool and silk threads. And what did he think of the title: The Fluid of the World? She wouldn't just welcome his suggestions, she actively wanted them. Then she slipped into a kind of sober sing-song, detailing everything she had to do before she left. Packing: the natural collection. Together with all the newly pressed snowdrops and heads of Christmas roses drying in Mesmer's tomes. Around ten flowers all in all. The *Hina ningyo* with its hair like silk didn't fit into her case. She'd hold it in her hand on the journey. Then the creatures she had to say goodbye to, the pigeons and the medicinal worms. The piano, which she'd really love to take with her, and the dog (which she'd also really love to take with her). Riedinger. And Kaline. And Anna and all those in the house endowed with five senses. And finally the man she's going to miss so much that she daren't imagine what this void will do to her soul . . . The man gifted with a sixth sense . . . Who's saved her on a number of occasions, from all sorts of things. Who this time, for the first time, is simply abandoning her . . . Him, the doctor. She gave a tortured smile and wiped her eyes.

He'd tried everything, he replied. Done his best. And her father would bring her back . . .

Did he believe what he'd believed from her father?

She hadn't waited for an answer. Had merely returned to her list-making. All the things in store for her. After the weekend in the country. When she got home. Home to the Rüssel.

Her two dear pianos. The warm welcomes. Koželuh,

Salieri, Metastasio. And surely she'd be meeting Herr von Kempelen soon. Maybe she'd get to play chess with the famous Turk. But first of all she'd play her *sicilienne* to Koželuh. At such a tempo that hearing and seeing would vanish. And then, she sang, she'd prepare for her tour. A major one throughout the whole of Europe. Travelling at least as far as the Mi-ma-mozart one. Maybe even further, who knows? To America . . . and on and on. To all the places she knew. Because her fingers had found them long ago on the spinning globe. Her trunk was now full and she'd sat on the closed lid, and he, he'd looped the leather strap around it.

He sees the people gathered in front of the house. Forming a chaotic cluster around the entrance. And the coachman confronting them. Negotiating. Raising his arms to appease them. Shaking his head. And the people moving into a phalanx. Pushing the helpless coachman into the house. This good man, who wasn't just trying to replace Kaline, but now Anna, too. Anna, who can create order like no other. She's probably escaped to a friend's house. Or she's gone to see Störck to put in a good word for him, her husband. And the good word had not fallen on deaf ears. It had been passed on. Until it had reached the most appropriate, most important ears. And so it happened that on the very evening before his departure Anna surprised him with a letter. A letter of recommendation from the state chancellor Prince Kaunitz to the empire's ambassador in France, Count de Merci-Argentau. For him, the doctor. For whose absence the dear old coachman is presumably trying to compensate (in vain).

With a cloth he wiped clean his old trunk, freeing it of cobwebs and dust. A job he would have left to Kaline in the past. And then he took five magnets from the wall. The heart-shaped one. The kidney-shaped one. The oval one. The round one. And the rod-shaped one. Not that the shape was significant. He hasn't believed this for a long time. The magnetic power is not dependent on something as obvious as the external form. Whoever ascribed this nonsense to him had misunderstood him. But experience shows that people have a more intense reaction to a heart than a shapeless lump. They don't know what a heart looks like of course. They've never seen one.

He'd packed the pieces in blue sheaths. And put them in his trunk which smelled of the cellar. A layer of felt on top. A layer of books. A layer of clothes. The purple suit. The grey one. A layer of instruments. The microscope. The electrostatic machine. He dismantled it. Then he decided that it must stay. The glass armonica, on the other hand, with all its individual fragile bowls. It would have been sensible to travel without it. But how could he do it without his glass armonica? It had to come with him. Even if he had to haul the thing single-handedly along the way. There are things he cannot be without.

He'd always thought that Anna was the one who was so attached to things. To things which cost something. He'd often reproached her for her profligacy. Whenever she came back with full bags from Vienna. And the coachman had to make at least eight trips to heave all the purchases to the front door. But when one day he'd dared suggest that she shouldn't get excessive with her shopping she'd exploded.

You, she screamed, you're attached to words. Especially the ones you don't have. That's no better!

But cheaper, he'd said, leaving her standing there with all her clobber. And heard her continue to scream behind him whether he wasn't aware that words were the most expensive things of all. Protected and tended by the scholars of the world. But she had no access to this world of words. And she'd hoped he might provide it for her. But of course it wasn't convenient for him. It was clear he had no interest in sharing his enigma with her.

Why was she saying that? he'd asked very calmly. What made her think that?

Because, she screamed, because secretly, he found her scary. The only one who'd taken her at face value, who'd ever done anything for her, was the lieutenant colonel . . .

He'd have gladly pursued this debate about her and him and language. Gladly answered all the reproaches. But when Anna started talking about her first husband he went doubly silent. His answer: A number two was never a match for a number one. Even she had this much understanding of mathematics. He'd stormed out of the room and hadn't sat down again the whole day. Not until the next one. And the one after the one after that. In the stagecoach.

And now, here, in his tiny room surrounded by water, his dry cell. He thinks of Baron von Störck, who'd called him a charlatan. A word that he had hung round him like a magnet too heavy for any Fluid of the World. It's unbearable. Even if, in this language which is spoken in Vienna, perhaps all it means is that he'll never set foot in academic paradise.

*

Watery noises spin around his head as if seeking an outlet. The stream, the current, the sea. He stands by the window. Feeling the sodden air from the mighty mill wheel on his skin. Breathing in all the all-penetrating spray. Breathing the flowing. The millstream. The power. Flushing him away. But he doesn't stop thinking. He's thinking, he thinks, and he will think further.

He will think without words.

✦⌇✦

What she needs here is a clear voice. As powerful and penetrating as the chorus of animals. The chorus of bees. The chorus of bumblebees, grasshoppers and crickets and flies. The chorus of female moths which are pestering her father especially (as in the Banat). To stand out from them, Maria speaks quietly. And much too softly.

Might she dictate something to him?

What is it, Resi?

A letter.

To whom?

Mesmer!

Please spare me this name. Why dwell on people that cause you harm?

He'd helped her.

She was imagining it.

Her imagination was one thing. That she wanted to ask the doctor something was another.

This is how it went on for days.

*

What else can she do but learn by heart the letter she's not permitted to dictate? Hoping that what has been learned by heart will find someone who will commit it to paper. At some point.

First, the opening: Gutenbrunn, May, Hello, dear Doctor Mesmer . . .

How can I express my gratitude? Gratitude for a reality which has now passed. And for this gift from your dear wife which is so alien here amongst cows and sheep and pigs. Your dear wife Anna, of whom I have such fond memories. She scarcely let go, she continued, of the *Hina ningyo*, this puppet with hair like silk. And whenever she played on the (toneless, dull) piano here, she either played it one-handed or sat the *Hina ningyo* where there wasn't any music. It's so soft and flexible. Just as I'd like to be, my dear, distant scientist. It's the *Hina* stroking me when I stroke it.

Her father cannot be convinced that the whole thing wasn't pure fantasy. And what she'd seen weren't merely images described to her. Not real, like the portrait on the wall. The whole thing one big deception that had shattered her nerves. That's how he puts it. Well, if her father says it then it must be true. And so from now on she's on the side of lies. That's the truth. Which I still have to get used to.

Hadn't her father seen her progress with his own eyes? And yet he says: Progress, that would be her playing again like she did before all this mumbo jumbo! That's what he was trying to achieve.

Maybe that, she answered immediately. But not any answers to my questions.

Only those relating to that fraudster, Resi, he'd insist on saying this again and again.

Dear, good, purple Mesmer, is it not understandable that I should prefer to be on the side of the things learned by heart, irrespective of what Riedinger thinks?

After they'd left for the hills far from Vienna she hadn't even tried to see. As soon as she was away from Mesmer, she'd closed her eyes and pulled over the layers of silk. She was keeping it like that whenever she could.

But it was no help against the snow-white milk, as her mother tried to talk it up, which she was forced to drink on a daily basis here to boost her health. It smells, dear Mesmer, of cow. (I can't close my nose, either.) And it tastes of cow. Yes, she knew he had great respect for animals. Because he considered them – they of course knew nothing – to be magnetic creatures. She was thinking about this today while standing in the meadow, singing her questions to the cows. She had felt smaller than small.

Her father refused to answer questions while she kept on singing.

He wondered whether he ought to consult Dr Störck for advice.

Was he trying to threaten her?

What, with milk and honey?

Every evening there's milk beside my bed and it goes cold.

She envied her time at the *palais* on the Landstraße. Today she realized that being able to say everything made it unnecessary to say everything. Maybe he was aware of this.

But why couldn't she ever realize things straight away,

rather than always in retrospect, when they were over?

Dear traveller – obviously travelling because of my blindness – what if at this very moment something sweeps past me which only when I'm back at the Rüssel I recognize as wonderful and missing from my life?

It seems to me as if I'm falling from one sleep into the next. From a dreamless, short sleep everybody's familiar with, into a deep, recuperative, balmy sleep, which everybody craves. And straight afterwards, there is no trill between them, into a dreaded, harsh, exhausting sleep.

It was precisely this which had clutched her in its iron grip over the past few days. Threatening to engulf her. Had already captured her dear *Hina ningyo*. Which, when she'd played it her *sicilienne* in a bad dream, had said it didn't believe that it was her *sicilienne*. And when she said, But I did compose it, the puppet laughed itself to death. But its eyes told me that it thought this piece was great, and some others besides. Great, great.

Dearest doctor, all she was longing for now was that bottomless, magnetic sleep in which you're alert and aware while you sleep.

He, the alert and aware one, surely knew about the sleep overwhelming her since Gutenbrunn.

But more of that later. Verbally. I hope.

Even though this letter was just swarming with questions. He didn't need to answer. Her father would never, ever allow a letter addressed to her from him.

❧ CHAPTER SEVENTEEN ☙

Paris, April, 1784

He who waits learns how to wait. There have been as many occasions over the last few years and months as there are poor people in Paris. Once he waited for an invitation from the Parisian Faculté des Médecins to demonstrate his method. Then he waited for the findings of a commission appointed by the government which was said to be interested in his method of treatment. The way the findings turned out meant that the waiting had not been worth it. But still. He waited.

Now he's waiting for an answer from a commission, appointed by King Louis XVI, which apparently is seriously examining his method. Men of the scientific calibre of a Franklin, a Lavoisier, a Guillotin. This time they'd understand. As he has understood that waiting is nothing but a space. A room with many doors. Which open in this or that direction, but open anyway. Like the door to his garden from his practice. Where he's planted flowers and medicinal herbs.

To begin with he waited for Anna's letters from Vienna.

For news from the Landstraße. About how the patients were and what the dog was up to. And always for Anna's response to his question: *When are you coming?*

And when, two months later, an answer arrived rather than Anna herself, it said that there had been such great progress in the patients' health that they had all flown. Back to the freedom of life. And the dog? It had gone, too. One day, following a storm, it had suddenly vanished. She'd called it, tried to get it to come, got them to search the woods for it. In vain. Either it had been the victim of a lightning strike or a bitch on heat. She thought the former was more likely, as she'd heard that this obsession with metal rods was spreading, taking over Europe, increasing in number along with the storms. But who could know? Love also struck like lightning sometimes. And maybe it'll come back, the little beast. She wasn't giving up hope. Just as she wasn't giving up hope that he, her husband, would come back.

For her answer to his final question had to be no, given the way everything was going. She certainly wouldn't be coming to Paris. She wanted to be with him, yes, more than anything in the world. With him in the Viennese world of the Landstraße.

Out of the question, he wrote. Here in Paris his work would be supported and funded. He was independent of his devotees. She must know, establishing good connections with better ones, with the very best connections. Kornmann was collecting money. To establish a society. A school of magnetism. A magnetic clinic.

227

She shouldn't imagine that he was lonely. Lonelier, perhaps, than if he knew nobody. The endless search for people who, like himself, were on a quest for the truth, was tiring. And always fruitless. It was as hard to find such people here as it was in Vienna. The whole of Paris a wasteland! A desert, peopled with creatures with no time for what is good. And mostly insensitive to his magnetic method as well.

Once more he waited over a month for an answer. Which then read: From everything she'd heard he was as much maligned in Paris as he was in Vienna. So surely it was no skin off his nose where the rain poured down on him. Whether he was here or there he was still maligned. And she with him. And if she could choose where she'd rather be maligned then rather in Vienna. She knew the city and its people.

Dear Anna, he wrote. French impoliteness is surely no less sour than its Viennese counterpart, but without question it's sophisticated.

He wrote how much he'd enjoyed her letters. But he'd stopped waiting for them. Now he was mainly waiting for the messengers. Bringing him correspondence from Kornmann and Bergasse. And one day he had in his hands a letter in which the banker, Kornmann, and the lawyer, Bergasse, told him that it was done. They'd assembled almost half a million. The monies came from all the provinces of France. Enough to set up a society, open a clinic and a magnetic school. In May La Société d'Harmonie de France will become reality.

For the first time the waiting has been worthwhile. Now that he's become an expert at waiting. He knew that, while waiting, everything possible was being done. Finding treatment rooms. Magnetising patients. Getting together a group of pupils. Drafting contracts, lucrative contracts. Appointing servants. And playing the glass armonica. And many French chickens were being cooked in an extremely spicy Parisian way, and French wines were being tasted as well. For Mesmer had waited so long that he'd allowed himself to forget he was waiting.

Until that day almost two weeks ago when he read in the paper that Maria von Paradis had arrived in Paris. To give a series of concerts.

She'd done it! She'd done it! Somewhere in a central region of his body there was jubilation: in the area around the *Solar plexus*. And (strangely), her triumph and his were knocking at the same Parisian door at the same time. As if they somehow belonged together. Even though he didn't believe in such forces of destiny.

Of course he will go along. He wants to see her. Definitely. And hear her.

In the days that follow, however, another thing becomes evident: he's waiting for a message from Maria. And waiting for Maria cannot be forgotten. It always makes its presence felt. Interferes in everything.

After accompanying the gouty Duchess de Chaulnes first through her complaints about gouty fingers, then to the baquet and, via a severe crisis, finally to the mattress room and thence to sleep, he was drawn again to the garden, out into the garden. Amidst the all-dominating lilac was the lungwort, in full bloom. The flowers are already beginning to close again. It is the afternoon. Nothing from Maria. This sort of waiting pains him. He is so pained that he no longer wants to go to the concert. He will miss it. Voluntarily. Even though he hasn't missed a single *concert spirituel* in Paris so far.

When the duchess finally wakes up, the lungwort has long since closed its blue flowers. Tomorrow they'll fall off, he thinks, hauling the heavy duchess up from the mattress. Her pains are gone, but she doesn't miss the opportunity to ask him whether he's still in contact with former patients.

That depends, he says.

On what?

On the circumstances. Why was she asking?

No particular reason . . . she says.

No particular reason?

Was he still in contact with that . . . *mademoiselle de Vienne?*

She'd read about it in the paper. Everybody had read about it in the paper. Anybody who reads the paper knows the story.

It runs: *Failed attempt by Monsieur Mesmer to cure the blind mademoiselle.* He'd already come across the story when he arrived in Paris years ago. This had been the doing of the crowd back in Vienna.

Do you mean, he says, Mademoiselle Paradis?

Yes, she said. The young blind girl . . .

You mean, he corrects her, the young blind girl who I saw see.

She's playing tomorrow evening in the Tuileries, in the Salle des Machines.

Yes, thank you. He read the *Journal de Paris*, too.

The Tuileries was only a short hop away. And five minutes if you used both legs. Was he going?

Of course, he lies.

Get there early, it'll be full, she says, very, very full.

It's good she's told him this.

He opens the door.

He's grateful to her.

This isn't a lie. He's eternally grateful that she's finally leaving his house.

Now it's just the pupils left. They're already sitting in a circle ready for their evening round table. There's a gap in the circle. Which he, Mesmer, has to fill. Opposite Bergasse. Flanked by Carra and d'Eslon. Brissot has given his apologies.

Pas de problème.

Lafayette, on the other hand, is there, and Puységur. There's no lack of ambition in the room. Nor of new experiences, either, after a long day of practical exercises ("*Allez, touchez, guérissez, messieurs.*") Which want to come out, to be reported, discussed, questioned. This is why he's sitting there. The master in the flesh. Who can't find peace in his flesh today. He could erupt with impatience. But in fact it's his pupils doing the erupting, chief among them d'Eslon, spouting a new, brand new experience.

Today he'd placed his hands on a young woman's stomach (which of course makes Mesmer think of Maria). He'd barely touched the stomach before she'd exploded . . . into a serious crisis.

Well, she was just sensitive, the young lady, says Mesmer who's desperate to leave the round table and its comments.

231

Maria might still ring. Last opportunity to call on him before the concert.

What's d'Eslon getting at?

He's convinced, he hears d'Eslon say, that the young woman didn't have a crisis as a result of his intervention, but through her own imagination. From now on, he says, he'll focus on this: on the power of imagination.

Mesmer says nothing. Stares at one pupil after another. Saying nothing. In the tension he calls d'Eslon's assertion a catastrophe. Proof of his shortcomings. Evidence that d'Eslon has learned nothing up till now. Absolutely nothing. Still a hopeless novice. He hasn't understood what it's about. This force. Universal force. The basis of his discovery is the Fluid which is transferred from person to person, even though this can't be verified by the measuring instruments available today. Anybody who sets out on their own without having understood the basis is misguided.

So concentrate on this, gentlemen. Or leave.

D'Eslon looks at him, dumbfounded.

The human imagination is also a strong force.

The pupils enter a discussion. Weighing up this point.

The master can't hear himself until he's bellowing. D'Eslon is arguing in exactly the same way as those doctors at the Paris faculty who failed to extend an invitation to him. The commission appointed by the king has still not convened. The Parisian authorities who, one after another, have swept animal magnetism from the table with a catalogue of words for no and once again no. As powerful as his speechlessness with regard to the big picture. Because they weren't able to measure the Fluid it didn't exist. Everything, he yells, every-thing is based on imagination. Untutored imagination.

Stop, d'Eslon shouts. This was precisely what he was trying to say.

But Carra shouts over him: Are they agreed that all the three institutions cited are elitist and hostile to the people? And that they don't need such institutions in the future?

Roaring approval.

Need to be got rid of.

More noise.

The effect of the moral on the physical is remarkably direct, Bergasse practically chokes. One might call it political. And anybody wishing to make it must acquire a secret.

D'Eslon shouts that he stands by his statement. The fact that Mesmer's method works is largely down to the imagination.

In all the hubbub Mesmer's protest cannot be heard. But something is filtering through to him. Amongst the cacophony of voices a sound reaches him: a soft minor third. The door-bell.

He stands up. Leaves the room. D'Eslon's voice is loud enough. To be heard everywhere. In the corridor, in the hall, at the door.

Mesmer's theory would be no less significant if imagination played the key role in it. That's where he differs from the members of the royal commissions. For him, sorry, I mean for me, the human imagination makes everything more interesting.

And he hears Puységur agree that there's something in that. But he at least believes that there's a force inside him.

That's where he gets the will to make it effective.

Carra manages to shout even louder. I believe that people can't help falling ill under immoral rule.

While his pupils drown each other out Mesmer opens the door, wide, as wide as he can.

Nobody. No Maria. Not even when he crosses the threshold and looks across the Place Vendôme. Where, in the sun-soaked shadows of the trees, two coaches rock in front of their shadowy shadows, stop, let out a few ladies who walk across the cobbles with their parasols – no Maria. Or is she there?

The power of imagination, he thinks. And wonders which Parisian hotel Maria is staying at. And fancies the Palais Royal. And whether she's feeling hounded by this big city as he was when he arrived years ago. Even arriving in the metropolis. This enthusiasm must be overcome. This growth in enthusiasm. He was blown away. Really blown away.

In Paris there was an impetus to walk. He had to walk continually.

Blown away. Walking to the opera. Walking to the Seine. Upstream. Downstream on the way back. Walking over the bridge, over to the other side. To the cathedral. And beyond. Through the winding alleys, the fluid odours. To the cathedral again. Walking up to Notre-Dame. From all directions and corners. Back to the river. Across again. To the Louvre. Towards the Tuileries. Through the park. He had to walk all day and all night as if this mad city had got into his legs, turned him into a machine that sucks everything up inside it. This incredible splendour and its incredible opposite. Everything was here as if it had been tipped out onto the street.

People offered their services at all times of day and night: their bodies, their powers, their discoveries. He would let people solicit him. In Vienna he would have moved on. Abroad he stopped. Marking time with his feet. Just as he was being given a chance here, he gave others one. First a fortune-teller who predicted more fame and wealth for him (let her be proved right). Then an individual who looked like a mix between a scientist and artist, sitting in a wicker chair above his beggar's hat and battered case. Through the thicket of his beard he was extolling the achievements dozing in this case.

Was Maria walking through the city? Would they recognize each other? Would she stop for a stranger? Would she be generous or thoughtless or lighthearted?

Mesmer had stood in front of these – as the bearded man asserted – ingenious inventions. Just loose pieces of paper, spread out in front of him, and prevented from flying away by a rustically broad hand. The plans to the machines which the ingenious man had constructed.

A machine that can fly without being a balloon. Without steam, without gas. Able to carry large weights, pump water, mill corn, propel itself. But it's not alive. Ever more puzzles on crumpled paper, spread out before Mesmer, served as proof. Ever more ideas: A new way of communicating over large distances. Completely without language.

Or the best of all: How to win over someone's heart in a trice, the heart of the one you love, someone you yearn for.

The final drawing, dashed off in a few, very scrawled lines, a device for seeing machines on distant planets in detail, as clearly as if they were here on earth.

How so?

Oh no! First of all twenty thousand livres and a roof over his head so that he can work on a few details in peace. Mesmer threw a coin into his hat. Said he had the same dreams. But the whole thing didn't seem to go beyond the wishing stage.

He'd walked on. So far that for the first time since his arrival he felt heaviness in his legs. And for the first time since his arrival he sat down. And from the marble steps in the Tuileries park he had watched two young women dressed in fashionable pink walk past him in conversation.

One cast a glance over at him, which immediately made his legs feel light again. He heard her say the name Guillaume and took her to be Kornmann's lover. She was exactly as he'd described her. Dark, lively locks of hair, and this bounteous, direct gaze.

Guillaume, pink said to pink, was sending her a new love poem every day. Or two. Honest rhyming dreariness. She'd let it be known that she'd only accept further poems if they were dressed in physics or metaphysics. Science was *en vogue*, and everything else was old hat.

Dreariness, that sounded just like Kornmann.

But poetry? No. Clearly there were quite a few sad Guillaumes in Paris. He was infected by the synchronized giggling of the two girls which set in all of a sudden. He's familiar with this sort of giggling from Maria. When she wants to laugh at something you're not supposed to laugh at. Because it's not funny, but pathetic. Maybe she's sitting in the Palais

Royal giggling to herself. Thinking of him, her old, infamous Mesmer.

He steps backwards into the house, carefully closing the door. He'll break up the round table. They'll all look at him in horror.

   The fact that he's entering the room means he'd gone away.

   Where was he?

   He doesn't answer.

   And how long?

   For as long as a concert, he'd like to answer. But he doesn't answer. He's all for silence. Which means he won't go to the concert. Under any circumstances.

⤜ CHAPTER EIGHTEEN ⤝

16 April, 1784

❦~❦

She turns, walks across the square. A princess in a dark-red dress, counting her paces. Twenty as far as the steps which lead up to the Palais des Tuileries. Inside people are waiting for her.

To celebrate her. The blind pianist. First and foremost her mother. Who's carried out important duties for the tour. She is reporter (on the time in Paris), Maria's eyes (in front of us the statue of Louis XIV, the genius of victory is holding the laurel wreath above his head). She is critical listener (Koželuh, fault-less. And played with feeling. Well done), Maria's chaperone (Riedinger!) and averter of perilous dangers such as draughts and sharp stones, as well as falling stones, direct sunlight, young men, old men and: Mesmer!

But she couldn't stop him from coming to the concert. She was sure that he'd come. Pop up as if from nowhere.

When she entered the cool dressing room from the cheering hall, someone in the room was breathing who hadn't been breathing before. Mesmer. Typical him.

Goodness gracious! She hadn't been expecting that!

She pretended to be surprised. Typical her. Lied. For his sake. Even though she hates lies as much as he does. As much as some people hate the truth. Or surprises. Or surprising truths. Everything that she and the doctor consider vital. The only difference being that he clearly prefers surprising other people. Whereas she likes being surprised as well as surprising, preferably both at the same time. What matters is that something is happening in her presence. Something astonishing. In which a living thing is fluttering. A hot air balloon rising up to the heavens or a deeply felt Haydn piece, a dog's moist snout or a warm, soft hand.

She was confused this time, too, when Mesmer gave her his hand. The elastic handshake grasped her right hand as if he were taking hold of Maria lock, stock and barrel. And she could have settled down as if in a comfortably padded nest.

The first thing Maria did was to push over her new notebook to him, so he could write something in it. And she asked him to read out what he had written. That was a mistake. Because straight away he asked her to open her eyes. Why did she have her eyes closed the whole time?

Out of habit, she said.

But people must think she's blind.

People, people.

You give them what they want so in the end you get what you want.

He thought that was wrong. You give them what you've got.

239

He might do that. He gave people what he had and nobody knew what it was.

Wrong, he said. His patients accepted what he gave them. She should try to remember.

Of course. But afterwards they don't know what they've been given. It can't be measured so precisely, either, she added.

But it can, he said. It was quite simple. The truth.

And she could see.

Hmm, she said.

Typical her. Lying for his sake.

She'd already proved it, he said.

Sometimes the world was clear and soft before her eyes, and then she disappeared again . . .

Her or the world? he interrupted.

How should I know? she retorted. What's certain is that nothing's certain. And that the world can disappear at any time and without any warning. And the disappearance and reappearance of the world disturbed her when she was playing. Whereas in the world of absence she could crack on uninhibited.

But she couldn't read, he said. It sounded scornful, like he had sometimes talked to Kaline. And then he read it out. Typical him.

On this evening he congratulated her from the bottom of his heart on her great musical triumph.

And she was surprised. Less by his words than by the tone of his voice. It was unfamiliar.

He was delighted! he said quietly, almost croaking, and his own voice contradicted him. It sounded bleak.

How were things with him? she said, immediately regretting the question. For her parents had regularly informed her of the public invective against him. She heard him approaching her and got out of the way. Not that he'd suddenly launched into his mumbo jumbo. Maybe he was taking a Spanish cane out of his bag, or a magnet. Just no experiments with her nerves right now.

She had to go straight back out again, to the audience, she said. Walked around the table. Riedinger would be calling her.

Riedinger? he groaned.

He was accompanying the tour, and her on the violin and generally . . .

She'd stepped behind the screen. She could hear him standing in front of it.

Was Riedinger choosing the music for her concerts, too?

No, she was doing that herself without any help.

He'd marvelled at her Haydn (piano concerto in G major), her enchantingly soft and silky playing. And she'd sung her song well (*I was a poor little worm*).

She'd reduced the whole room to tears, even in the French translation.

She hadn't noticed any of that, she said. Everything that happened before her in the hall flowed straight back into her playing.

But there was one thing he didn't understand, he said. She could have played Mozart, but she played Koželuh instead.

The people preferred listening to Koželuh.

That wasn't a reason. But, oh well. He liked it anyway.

As for her, she said. She'd never been so pleased. It was

almost frightening how pleased she was right now. As if she might die of it.

She was thinking that, he said, because she'd reached her goal.

And she: She hadn't reached it. Not yet. Her goal was Versailles. She wanted to be invited. By the king. Play a concert in the Grande Salle. Be applauded as she had been here.

She had a chance, he replied softly. He'd seen the king in the hall.

And the queen, she said.

The fact that they're there, he replied. And her mother enthroned beside the queen.

Her mother would live off that for the rest of her days. The less her mother saw of him the better, she added. She didn't want him to return to the hall.

Not to worry. He'd sat behind a woman with a fashionable balloon hairdo, his nose had been full of powder.

She'll remember the hairdo he went on to describe. There were tiny balloons attached to the tresses as well, one of which even had a basket. In it the Montgolfier brothers – brightly painted lead figures. Their arms stretched out to the heavens. She'll amaze the whole of Vienna with this.

They let him in without any fuss, he said. He's known here.

Of course. Where wasn't he known? It's known all the way to Vienna that he's known here. It doesn't matter where Mesmer lives, people know him. He's noticed always and everywhere. An exotic bird. And where in the world do they not pounce on exotica?

When he'd entered the hall, he said, whole rows of people turned their heads.

But she didn't notice a thing. She was too preoccupied. Composing herself before the concert. Of course he didn't believe a word of this. How could he? She was on the side of lies. The moment she opened her mouth and talked of something other than being pleased. But some lies are more honest than the truth.

She gently lifts her red dress and starts climbing the stairs.

He claimed that her head had turned towards him, too. But not like the other people. More like a flower turning to the sun.

And all of a sudden she was unable to contain her laughter. She could hardly breathe, but not because of what he'd said, not at all. She'd merely laughed. She wasn't paying attention. When she doesn't pay attention she laughs. Just as a hot air balloon will rise into the sky if you don't hold onto it. That's what her laughter was like. It was all to do with this evening. The place. And the unending applause. The position of the stars and his Fluid.

She'd stepped out from behind the screen and sat down at the table. When he sat down, too, she thought that this was the first time a table had been exactly the right size for the two of them.

Her sun, she said across the table, was music, which she heard before she even struck the first note. She hadn't noticed him.

Well, he was happy. That she hadn't noticed him.

Why was he speaking so softly?

He wasn't speaking softly.

243

No?

No, he replied even more softly.

But he should have every reason to be pleased. She really ought to congratulate him.

Why?

On his writing?

Which writing?

Riedinger had read some of it to her. Thanks to that little book she'd understood his theory for the first time, she said.

Which book?

The one about his work. And what a great idea to give it a woman's name. She begged to be forgiven if she couldn't remember the exact title . . . something with *magnetic*, obviously and *truth*, she said.

What truth?

Oh, *Madame Henriette de Barbe-bleu*, she said, sensing him flinch again already.

What was she talking about?

Printed in Strasbourg, bound in the finest blue on blue marbled paper.

He'd neither written nor published such a thing.

Not under his name, not under a different name and certainly not under a woman's name. Regrettably, he practically whispered, she'd . . .

Anybody who believes it . . . she whispered back, and was glad that Riedinger called at that very moment.

Quick, she had to go. To play piano.

What do you wish for? she called to him over her shoulder.

She shouldn't have asked that. She might have expected that he'd wish for the impossible.

Mozart with open eyes.

In the corridor she touched Riedinger's hand quivering with excitement and then let go again soon afterwards.

Don't go out yet, he whispered, wait another minute. The longer you keep them waiting the more they'll love you.

She didn't want to think about that now, but stopped by the door and waited anxiously. She could hear the applause gradually dying down. A few people, three or four, were still clapping. Rapidly and vigorously, as if they wanted to make up for those who'd stopped.

Behind her she could hear the doctor greeting her Riedinger. And her Riedinger was mightily surprised. Just as she was when she heard him asking the doctor for help. He needed to send a package.

What kind of package?

He didn't have the time to arrange the dispatch.

And she listened, sharing Mesmer's astonishment. A package to Kaline. And what was in it?

A very interesting question! So interesting that she now heeded Riedinger's advice. What could Riedinger be sending from Paris to Kaline in Vienna?

She'd love to know. Still.

Something tiny, he said. And: A long story. And all very awkward, the whole thing.

All very awkward. Now she was a part of it, too. And suddenly her performance seemed awkward, too. The last ones applauding had clapped in a rhythm that anticipated the rhythm of her footsteps. A clapping which was trying to draw her onto the stage. She could have let herself go along with it. But she wanted to stay in the conversation. In which the doctor was enquiring about Kaline's child.

And Riedinger said she'd had it. The boy was getting on well. No surprise there. Brought into the world according to Mesmer's instructions. Kaline had fought like a lion. He knew this from Hossitzky who'd ended up marrying Kaline. Now she's got four. The first one, two others and Hossitzky.

She heard the men laugh. Barely able to distinguish between them. And would have loved to laugh herself. But go onto the stage laughing? According to her far-sighted mother a blind pianist was more serious than serious, and people had to see her looking that way. That was what people had to hear. And what was heard was what people said about her. She broke away from the laughter and walked slowly, gracefully towards the mounting applause.

When her greatest wish had come true, she found the doctor alone at the table. Even though he congratulated her again, she couldn't feel any happier.

It merely struck her that, just as her eyes which were used to darkness felt all light as pain, maybe the doctor felt her success as pain. And she decided not to tell him that afterwards the king had invited her for a drink.

All she said was that she was tired. And she was, too. She'd never thought that happiness could be so exhausting. And incidentally, the Emperor Joseph had cancelled her honorary pension. But now she was desperate for some fresh air. Would he accompany her outside?

He got up. She followed him through the corridor and several other rooms towards the exit.

What a shame, he said, that she couldn't see this splendour.

And she: Her mother, her eyes, had already described it all to her. She was very impressed by all the gold and the paintings. By the way, she added in a whisper, if the afore-mentioned eyes happen to cross their path, he had to make himself invisible immediately. On no account was her mother to see them together.

She could hear him clearing his throat and wasn't sure if he'd understood her.

Because he started talking about his practice. Which had such splendid rooms, he said, with purple silk walls. Patients and pupils streamed in and out every day.

He'd since realized that the world of science was not ready for his discovery. He was now focusing on teaching and practice. He didn't need judges any more. He needed pupils. And he had them. They met each day in the old palace at Place Vendôme No. 16.

The window shutters and lamps could be adjusted with such subtlety that he could produce every nuance of light and darkness any time of the day or night.

Whenever the doctor waxes lyrical he doesn't stop.

Lovely, she said. Lovely, lovely, lovely.

Until she said it no longer. Was not even amazed any more. By the luxury coaches his patients arrived in. The musical servant who greeted them at the door and would signal to the doctor by varying the tone of his whistle how important the person was who had just entered the house and was approaching the magnetic baquet.

It all sounded so different from what she knew in Vienna.

Did he have music in his practice as in Vienna?

Music? he said. An entire orchestra. Six violins, a viola, an oboe, a French horn.

Every day?

Every day. And of course the glass armonica. He played that himself. And a pianoforte. An original Silbermann. Did she perhaps . . . ?

No, unfortunately not. The time when she'd have had time for it was over. Tomorrow she was going to Versailles and . . .

Energetic footsteps on high heels which were making a rapid approach. The distances in this palace are long, but she feared they were far too short. She knew the hand which was now patting her cheek.

There she was, her mother said. They were waiting for her. Salieri. And Herr von Kempelen who was travelling around Europe with his chess Turk and staying in Paris at the moment. And countless French people.

She was to wait for her here, she wanted to freshen up a little, the mother said.

The tottering footsteps went away as energetically as they had arrived.

She'd gone out through the door. Breathing in and out deeply. And searched for him. For his footsteps, his voice. Had sniffed the air like an animal in the wind. Wished for alert, skilful eyes. Then she'd walked down the steps and crossed Place Louis XV.

But didn't find him.

She turns around, walks back across the square. A princess in a dark-red dress, counting her paces.

Twenty as far as the steps which lead up to the Palais des Tuileries.

Behind her a coach departs, eight hooves rattle away, another one arrives, sixteen hooves are brought from a trot to a pace, stop. People get out. Pieces of luggage thrown onto the street. Somewhere four paws are clicking across the Parisian cobbles. A woman shouts, *Attention!*

And a man's voice, *Mon Dieu! Le Diable!*

She moves away from the bustling noises of Paris. Slowly climbs the stairs. Pleased that the doctor was there. And that he's gone again. And about her concert. And the evening. And her happiness. And something wet touches her hand which she pulls away at once. The wet, soft, sniffling thing dancing around her, getting caught in her clothes, almost falls down the steps. Almost taking her with it.

A man's voice gets closer. She should watch out. They're never going to get rid of this black devil. It's been following him for weeks. And he swears to God it's not his dog.

Nor hers, she calls back.

And he: But it's behaving as if it is. The best thing would be if he shot it. Here and now.

No, no, she shouts. She knows where it belongs.

The dog which can't help sneezing and sneezing again in its delight follows her to where the coaches are. No sooner has she opened the door to the coach than it leaps in before her. She strokes its matted fur, smells her hands, rubs its soft ears between her fingers until it stops panting and lies down, its head on its paws. Its nose snuggles up to her satin shoes. When she gets up it lifts its head. She jumps out of the carriage, shutting the door from the outside. Place Vendôme No. 16. The coachman has understood.

ALISSA WALSER is a novelist, translator and painter living in Frankfurt am Main. She is the author of three volumes of short stories, one of which won the prestigious Ingeborg Bachmann Prize. *Mesmerized* was the winner of the 2010 Spycher Literaturpreis in its original German edition.

JAMIE BULLOCH's translations include *Portrait of a Mother as a Young Woman* by F. C. Delius, *Ruth Maier's Diary*, *Love Virtually* by Daniel Glattauer, and novels by Paulus Hochgatterer and Martin Suter.